THUG ME THE RIGHT WAY

DIAMONDATL

NAI

URBAN AINT DEAD

URBAN AINT DEAD PRESENTS

Thug Me The Right Way

By DiamondATL & Nai

URBAN AINT DEAD

P.O Box 448
Maybrook, NY 12543

Cover Design: P. Wise / The Wise Services

Edited By: Veronica Rena Miller / Red Diamond Editing by V. Rena, LLC

reddiamondediting5@yahoo.com

responsibility for errors or omissions. Neither is any liability assumed for damages resulting from the use of the information contained herein. This is a work of fiction. Names, characters, places, and incidents are either the product of the author's imagination or are used fictitiously. Any resemblance to actual events, locales, or persons living or dead is entirely coincidental.

Contact Author on IG: @diamondatl

Contact Author on FB: Authoressnai / IG: @authoressnai / TikTok: @authoressnai / Email: hoodloverssociety@gmail.com

Contact Publisher at www.urbanaintdead.com

Email: urbanaintdead@gmail.com

ISBN: 979-8-9888415-7-9

CONTENTS

SOUNDTRACKS

Scan the QR Code below to listen to the Soundtracks/Singles of some of your favorite U.A.D titles:

Don't have Spotify or Apple Music?
No Sweat!
Visit your choice streaming platform and search URBAN AINT DEAD.

Currently on lock serving a bid?
JPay, iHeartRadio, WHATEVER!
We got you covered.

Simply log into your facility's kiosk or tablet, go to music and
search URBAN AINT DEAD.

URBAN AINT DEAD

Like & Follow us on social media:
FB - URBAN AINT DEAD
IG: @urbanaintdead
Tik Tok - @urbanaintdead

SUBMISSIONS

Submit the first three chapters of your completed manuscript to urbanaintdead@gmail.com, subject line: Your book's title. The manuscript must be in a .doc file and sent as an attachment. The document should be in Times New Roman, double-spaced, and in size 12 font. Also, provide your synopsis and full contact information. If sending multiple submissions, they must each be in a separate email. Have a story but no way to submit it electronically? You can still submit to URBAN AINT DEAD. Send in the first three chapters, written or typed, of your completed manuscript to:

URBAN AINT DEAD
P.O Box 448
Maybrook, NY 12543

DO NOT send original manuscript. Must be a duplicate.
Provide your synopsis and a cover letter containing your full contact information.
Thanks for considering URBAN AINT DEAD.

Kaia

"Girl, get up before you're late for school!" I heard my mother yell from the hallway as she passed through, getting ready for work, I'm sure. Throwing my pillow over my head, I screamed into it. *I just need five more minutes, just five, Lord. Talk to ya girl.* "Kaia Monique Phillips, get yo' ass up before I have to physically remove you from that bed!"

"Okay, Ma. Dang, always tryna get violent." The last part of my statement I made sure to say under my breath. Diane Phillips was nothing to play with. She didn't care that I thought I was grown because I'd just turned eighteen last weekend, she didn't take no shit. Today was my official last day of high school before I graduated next week. Thank God for small favors.

Words couldn't describe how happy I was to leave high school behind. And I had a vast vocabulary, so that said a lot. I was over the teachers, students, janitors, even the lockers. You name it, I was over it. I had dreamed of this day the moment I ended my freshman year. It was time to move on to the next chapter in my life.

Rolling over in my queen-sized bed, I dreaded the thought of having to get out of my twelve hundred thread count sheets and the Tempur-Pedic mattress that lulled me to sleep every night. Sitting up straight, I gave my body a much-needed stretch. Closing my eyes, I thanked God for allowing me to see another day, climbed out of bed, and slipped my feet into my Ugg slippers. Before I could make it to the bathroom, my bedroom door was slightly pushed opened.

"Hey, Stink, you decent?" My sister, Kristen asked through the cracked door with her hand covering her eyes.

"Yes, fool. Come in." I laughed. "I'ma 'bout to hop in the shower." Kristen entered with a big smile on her face and sat down at the desk, next to my bed. "Whatever it is you're about to ask, the answer is no, Bookie." I knew that smile all too well. She either wanted me to sketch something for her to wear or go on a date with her. And let me say, I'd much rather sketch the fit for her and sew.

"Ahh Stink, don't act like that," she dragged out while

wrapping her arms around me. "Go take ya shower and I'll tell you wassup once you're out."

"Yeah, uh huh. I'ma let you get it out, but I just feel that my answer is still gonna be no. Mommy leave yet?"

"How you tryna kick me out of my own house?" My mother appeared at my door, fully dressed with her coffee and keys in hand. "Oh, hey stranger, you remembered you had a mama on this beautiful Friday morning?" She playfully chastised Kris before walking in and kissing her cheek. Ever since Kris had moved out a year ago, my mother complained about seeing less and less of her.

"Don't do me like that, Ma. You know I love you. I've just been really busy at the shop lately," Kris said in her defense to which my mom responded with an, "mmhmm."

"I'll be back late tonight, Kaia, so order in. Mase left some money on the table for you. I'll see y'all later, love you." Hugging us both, she left out. My mother was such an inspiration and the epitome of a hard-working woman.

Notice I said, "hard working woman" and not hard-working *black* woman. People kill me wanting to put color on everything. My mother worked as a Charge Nurse at Presbyterian Hospital and had been there for the past ten years. She was such a beautiful woman inside and out. I could never understand how my sperm donor fucked that up.

Kris and I knew exactly who our sperm donor was, he just acted as if he didn't know us. Honestly, it was absolutely fine by me. I considered Mase my dad anyway. Mase was my mom's fiancé. They'd been together for five years and were newly engaged as of six months ago.

He went all out for his proposal, too, making sure to include me and Kristen in ever little detail. He'd been solid since the beginning. Mase gave me and Kris the space to come to him, which helped to build our bond organically. He treated us like queens and for that, he was A1 in my book.

Once my mom left, I made my way to the shower. Being late wasn't an option, even if it was my last day. By the time I was fully dressed in my black slacks and school polo it was seven forty. I had to be out the door by eight to get to school by eight thirty. Happy that Kris was still here, I knew I could catch a ride with her.

"Okay sis, I'm ready, and you have the pleasure of driving me to school."

Looking up from her phone, she smiled. "Oh, the joys of life."

I gave her smart ass the finger. Pulling off my silk scarf, I unwrapped my fresh blow out and let my hair fall nicely pass my shoulders. I had a head full of thick hair that could only be tamed by my stylist and cousin, Heaven.

"Oh yes sister, Heaven did her big one," Kris praised while I brushed my hair, making sure there were no fly aways.

"I know, right. We had a little hiccup at first when she called herself tryna cut it in layers. Ol' scissor happy ass." Giggling, Kris stood up, letting me know she was ready.

Applying a coat of Fenty gloss to my lips, I grabbed my MCM book bag, and jean jacket and was ready to go.

"Don't forget your money, Stink," she reminded me, while walking to the door.

Grabbing the hundred-dollar bill from the kitchen counter, I checked its authenticity in the light and nodded.

"Why you checking the money, Kaia?" She laughed, standing at the door.

"Cause, me and Mase been having prank wars for the last week. Last night, I emptied out his whole Casamigos bottle and added water to it." Just thinking about his face when he poured himself a shot had me rolling.

"No, you didn't." Kris cracked up laughing.

"Yes, I did. So, I gotta be careful around here. I can't be walkin' round with no funny money." Slipping the money into my wristlet, I continued on to the door.

"Stuff like that makes me miss home."

"Don't let mommy hear you say that. You'll go back to your apartment and find the U-Haul people witcho shit packed and ready to go."

We both got a good laugh out of the truth in my joke and headed out the door to her new Mercedes AMG truck. I lived comfortably in a brownstone on the Westside of Harlem. With no traffic, my school was a twenty-minute drive. Spring was coming to a close and Summer had crept through, allowing us to ride with the windows down.

"Okay, so what you wanted to talk to me about, Kristen?" I turned a little in my seat to face her.

"Oh, don't hit me with the full first name." She smirked and I did the same. She knew I was on to her ass.

"Okay, so you know Maine, right?"

I looked at her with a raised brow, who didn't know Maine? He was famous on the battle rap scene and known to make moves in the streets. "Yeah, I know of him. Why, wassup?"

"Well, it turns out he's Ant's brother and seeing as though we're going on our first date, I was thinking..."

"Ahh hell naw," I cut her off before she could continue. "Nope, nah, uhn uhn. You always do that, Kristen. You can't go on just one damn date by yourself?" I already knew the answer to my own question; I don't know why I even bothered asking.

"You know the first date has to be a double date to feel him out. If you don't like him, I don't date him." It was that simple for her. We were two peas in a pod. Although she was three years older than me, we had always been on the same level mentally and she valued my opinion.

"You lucky I love you, chick," I said, conceding, without much of a fight. "Where we going?" Low key, I was crushing on Maine. I had never spoken to him, but I'd seen him around a handful of times and baby boy was something special. Standing at six foot one with a low fade, he was the definition of *waves on swim, so they hate on him.* His butterscotch skin tone complimented my bronze glow. I just knew we'd make pretty babies. Finding out he was Ant's brother was quite a surprise.

Ant, short for Antwon, was a big deal in the streets. He had been trying to get close to Kris for a while now. In the beginning of the chase, she was fresh off of a breakup with her ex, Kane. That was one fucker I could not stand. I was still holding onto the hope that he'd go to sleep one day and never wake up. I liked the fact Ant was persistent in the chase. My sister deserved all the happiness in the world.

"Hello, earth to Kaia. Did you hear anything I just said?" She snapped her fingers at me.

"You want me to lie?" I fired back with a smirk, making her mush me.

"You so ignorant yo'. What I said was, we're going to Clyde Fraziers. Ant don't believe we can ball."

"They never do," we said in unison. It was true, nobody believed we knew how to play basketball because of how prissy we appeared to be. It was one of the two things our sperm donor had taught us. How to play ball and that niggas ain't shit, him being the prime example.

"I'll let him know we're on for next Friday night, cool?" I nodded my confirmation. "Good, now get outta my car." We'd pulled up in front of my school quicker than I thought. Loosening my seatbelt, she playfully nudged me to get out.

"Girl please, I've been kicked out of better places." Sticking my tongue out at her, I closed the door.

"Yeah, okay, keep that same energy when you wanna borrow it." Now she was getting carried away.

"Okay, okay sorry and I love you." I quickly back-pedaled, knowing at some point during the summer, I planned on stunting in her car.

"Yeah, I bet. Have a good day, love you, too."

With that, she drove off, leaving me to face the day. *Alright Kaia, this is the last day before graduation, you can do this.* I had to coach myself before stepping into the building. I wondered if my girls, Mecca and Shanice had the same slow start as me this morning. Who am I kidding? We all felt the exact same way about school. We were past the point of ready.

Mecca and Shanice were cousins who couldn't be more different personality wise and in the way they were raised. Mecca liked to be in the mix, and with her mom not being as strict as mine, she was able to rip and run until her heart was content. Shanice, on the other hand, was similar to me. While we were both very social, there were certain things our parents weren't letting us do. Either way, we blended well, and I wouldn't change my crew for the world.

From the freshmen to the seniors, everybody knew us. Each one of us gave main character energy. Some people loved it and others hated from the sideline. And that was a good thing because my attitude was something vicious. One of those sideline haters was Kandice Thompson.

I just knew the mere thought of me, made her mad. It

showed anytime we were in the same space. I was a vibe and in a class of my own. I didn't do too much and even still; I posed a threat. Shit, if I was her, I'd probably hate me, too. Putting on a welcoming smile, I got ready to tackle the last day.

"GIRL, WAKE UP, CLASS IS OVER," I whispered harshly while shoving Mecca awake. Our AP History class had just ended and she'd slept through most of it.

"Aight, I'm up. This class so goddamn boring. I'm glad it's over and done with." She stretched and straightened out her clothes.

"While you at it, cuz, get that drool on the side of your mouth." Leave it up to Shanice to make a joke.

"Bitch, shut up, acting like yo' ass wasn't sleeping, too." Mecca laughed, balled up a piece of paper, and threw it at Shanice.

"Beauty sleep, baby, beauty sleep," Shanice countered, using her compact mirror to make sure her face was good.

"Beauty sleep my ass, both y'all hoes was knocked out. Come on before we late for Mrs. Battaglia's class." I got up to walk out, and they followed.

"Yes ma'am," they responded in unison. The one class we didn't play about was English. Mrs. B was a beast, but she was my favorite teacher. Her class just so happened to be one of two classes I had with Kandice's crooked letter I shaped ass.

"Alright, ladies and gentlemen, being that this is your last day in my class, I'd like to give out some awards I personally created," Mrs. B announced once we all were seated.

"Y'all sit back and keep it cute cause you know we each have our name on one of those awards," I let both Mecca and Shanice know. They nodded in agreement.

I didn't hang with dummies; my girls were just as smart and talented as me. As Mrs. B called out different names, just as I predicted, my girls collected one each. By the time she'd gotten to the last name, I was on the edge of my seat.

"This last award goes to a student who has surpassed my expectations with her writing skills and dedication to the arts."

"Come on Mrs. B, give my girl her award so she can make these hoes sick," Mecca jumped up from her seat and blurted out.

"Have a seat, Shamecca, and watch your language," Mrs. B scolded.

Holding her hands up, she sat back down. "My bad, my bad, do you." The class snickered and so did Mrs. B. She was used to Mecca's outbursts and antics.

"As I was saying, this student has done her *big one*, as you all say. I'm happy to present this award to Kaia Phillips." Getting up to receive my award, I moved with style and grace as the class clapped and congratulated me.

"Yess, go friend! Y'all better show out for my girl, haters included," Shanice implored while looking in Kandice's direction.

I gave Mrs. B a quick hug and accepted the small plaque. "First, I'd like to thank the Academy..." The class roared in laughter and I giggled before continuing. "Nah, forreal though, thank you Mrs. B for acknowledging my skills and helping me perfect my writing. I also want to thank all of you for being great material as well." Throwing up the peace sign, I sashayed back to my desk.

The rest of class was a breeze and that was appreciated. The bell rang and we were off to the next.

"Aight y'all, three more classes to go and we out this nasty." I was so geeked.

"Yes, I can't wait to cut up this weekend like, *Mecciana, 'bout to graduate high school, graduiana.*" Even though the last part sounded dumb, Shanice and I joined in, doing the buss down dance with her.

"Ayee, buss down graduiana, I wanna see you buss down." We laughed, hyping each other up until I felt myself getting bumped. "What the fuck!" I yelled and turned around. My eyes instantly landed on Kandice and the two pitbulls she hung out with. I didn't refer to them as pitbulls to be funny either. Her friends were really strong in the face. I was convinced that Kandice only hung out with them because she was prettiest out of the trio. "You just couldn't wait until after graduation to get yo' ass whipped, huh? You want your black eye expedited," I threatened, handing my book bag to Mecca.

"Bitch, please. I wouldn't even waste my time. Come on y'all, ghetto is contagious." Her scary ass walked off once she saw the crowd forming.

"Friend, just let me beat her ass for you," Mecca offered. "Unlike yo' mama, all mine gon' ask when the school call is if I won." She handed me back my bag and I held it in the hook of my arm.

"Right. Aunty Rita be cuttin' up," Shanice cosigned. "Kandice ain't worth yo' time though, friend. She just mad cause her nigga still checking for you. Come on so we can finish out this day."

We moved about the hallways, to our next class without incident. Kandice's beef with me went back to our freshman year, on our second day of school.

I had just walked into the cafeteria, in search of a table for me and the girls to sit at. They'd stayed behind in math class a few extra minutes to discuss the syllabus. Finally finding a table amongst the crowd, I sat down and pulled out my phone to keep me occupied.

"Hey, beautiful, how'd you manage to smuggle yo' phone in here?" I looked up to see who was talking to me and took note of the hazel eyed cutie who stood in front of me. He put me in the mind of Omarion's brother, O'Ryan, only taller with a low-cut fade.

Snickering, I responded. "I didn't smuggle anything in. I

walked in with my phone like the gangsta I am." I flexed, making him laugh.

"Oh, aight, gangsta. What's your name?" He asked, taking an unoffered seat.

"So, you bold, huh? You just gon' sit down without asking, okay. My name is Kaia, and you, bugaboo?" I joked.

"Aaron. I see you got jokes, gangsta."

"A lil' something, something." We sat and chopped it up until the girls showed up. They introduced themselves and we continued to talk throughout the lunch period. As we were leaving out, Aaron asked for my number. Before I could shoot him down, his name was called from across the cafeteria.

*"**Aaron!**" The female voice called out with much aggression before walking over with two girls behind her.*

"Looks like you got some company, bugaboo." I was cursing his smooth-talking ass out in my head, but my face remained straight.

The girl grilled me before going in on Aaron who looked uninterested. Not one for drama due to my hands having a mind of their own, I removed myself from the equation. I wasn't for the goofy shit. It just so happened that the same girl was in my fifth period class. This was the one class I didn't have with Shanice and Mecca. As I maneuvered around the seats, I found one to my liking near the window. Pulling out my books, I prepared to get my learn on.

"Listen, I know you're new here and all, but Aaron is off limits, okay?" The girl stood over me, staking claim to her so-called man.

*"We all new here, sis. We're freshmen, remember? Meaning we all just started. And instead of coming to me, let **him** know that **I'm** off limits as well. Now, you're invading my personal space, and it's making me feel threatened. Soon, I'ma feel like I have to protect myself." Pushing back from the table, I let her know in not so many words that I was with the shits.*

"Yeah, aight," was her weak ass response before walking away. I knew a scary bitch when I saw one and Kandice was the scariest.

That's where it all started and still, Aaron had been on my bumper every chance he got. He was well aware that his ass had been friend zoned and it still didn't stop him. We had finally completed our last class and I couldn't be more ecstatic. We were getting our cap and gowns at the graduation, so at this point, we were free to roam the streets.

"Yo', y'all coming to my farewell party tonight?" Aaron pulled up on us as we congregated at my locker. His question was posed to the group, but he stared directly at me.

"Farewell party? Where you going, boy?" I inquired.

"You ain't know? I got accepted to USC, baby," he announced with a Kool-Aid smile on his face.

"Ahh, I forgot they announced that. I didn't think you'd be leaving so soon. Give me a hug, bugaboo, I'm gonna miss your annoying ass." Pulling him in for a hug, my body tingled as he squeezed me tight. Although I hadn't given him any play, I was still very attracted to Aaron. Not only was he fine, but smart as hell and an all-around athlete. I was genuinely happy for him.

"Well damn, how long y'all gon' hug for?" Hearing Shanice, I quickly broke our embrace and he shot me a sly smirk.

"Hater," he joked.

Confirming our attendance, I locked arms with the girls, we walked off. It was time to plan for how we were gonna kill this party. Instead of going straight home, we headed to Mecca's house. Her house was always lit on Fridays due to her mom's weekend card games with her homegirls. We rode the train to Concourse Village, in the Bronx, and walked the two blocks to her house.

"Look, before we go in here, I want y'all to know my mama is trying out a new look." We looked at Mecca confused but let her continue. "Don't y'all *dare* laugh. Matter fact, don't even comment on it, got it?" We both nodded. I had a feeling she was being over the top, so I ignored her. She opened the door and the smell of chicken frying hit my nose, making my stomach growl.

"That you, Mecca?" Her mom called out from the kitchen.

"Yeah, Ma. Kaia and Sha here, too, so I hope you're decent." Ms. Lynn was known to wear some crazy things and would cuss you out if you had something to say about it.

"Girl, please, this my damn house. You lucky I ain't ass naked. Hey, my soon to be graduates." She came out of the kitchen and I legit had no words. Respectfully, I returned the hug she gave me while mouthing, *"what the fuck?"* to Mecca, who just shook her head. Ms. Lynn had platinum blonde finger waves in her head and had topped it off with gold glitter.

As if on cue, Shanice started her aunt up. "Yess, aunty, come through serving the people a blonde moment." She spun her around and Ms. Lynn posed like she was killing the game. It wasn't the style that got me, but the color choice on her midnight complexion had me blown. Once Shanice was done giving her props, we headed to Mecca's room.

"Sha, you know you ain't shit," I said before busting out laughing. Sha held her stomach from laughing so hard.

"Y'all stop clowning my mom," Mecca scolded us, trying not to crack up herself.

"Aight, I'm done, but you need to tell yo' mama that's not the style for her. She walking around here looking like an extra in an Uncle Luke video." I couldn't stop myself from falling out in a fit of giggles again. "Okay, I'm done, I'm done forreal this time." I got myself together and focused on helping her pick out what she would wear to the party. We were celebrating Aaron and most importantly, being a part of the graduating class of 2020.

Kristen

I was elated that my sister agreed to go on this date with me. My suitor, Antwon, had been more than persistent, and I would've hated to have let him down for the fourth, time. He'd become a breath of fresh air after my tumultuous relationship with my ex, Kane that ended a while ago. No one could've told me that my relationship with the man of my dreams would consist of multiple black eyes and secret trips to the hospital. The only people who knew about my struggle was my sister and my cousin, Heaven.

My last encounter with Kane was the last straw. We got into a heated argument about his close relationship with his so-called "best friend" China. They were too damn close.

And even after telling him in the beginning that I didn't play the best friend shit, he still allowed her to call all times of the night, complaining about her relationship or to shoot the shit. Any sane woman would call their homegirl if they were having relationship issues, not the next woman's man. And calling my man between the hours of 11 p.m. and 3 a.m. only tells me you fucking him or want to. It was simple *girl math* to me.

We got into it bad one night over her spending the night and him neglecting to tell me. I happened to pop up one morning and there she was, on his couch, in his t-shirt, eating a bowl of cereal. All logic went out the window as I pounced on her stupid ass. I let out all my pent-up frustration and hurt from Kane beating my ass on her. Of course, instead of coming to my defense, he came to hers instead.

One thing led to another, and I woke up in the hospital with a bandage on my head and no recollection of how I got there. Kaia and Heaven were asleep in the uncomfortable chairs, and I was confused. By the time they awoke, I was still racking my brain, trying to piece the night back together. Heaven was the first to clear everything up for me, letting me know that Kane had hit me so hard during the altercation, that I became unconscious. He'd called Heaven and told her to meet him at the hospital, where he had dropped me off.

I could do nothing but cry and feel sorry for myself. My mama didn't raise me to be anyone's punching bag and at that very moment, I knew it was over for me and Kane. He never showed up to the hospital during my overnight observation and I was fine with that. I ended up being hospitalized for two whole days with my sister and Heaven in my ear, threatening to cut me off if I went back to him. I knew they would never really cut me off, but they had to say something to get my attention and they got it. While I had healed physically one hundred percent, I had was only healed about seventy five percent mentally.

I met Antwon when he came into my salon to get his dreads re-twisted.

He swaggered in on a blistering winter day in his Canadian Goose coat with the big hood covering his head. His Balmain jeans hung just below his waistline, showing his Ethika boxers. On his feet were a fresh pair of Timberland boots. He was just the way I liked my men— thugged the fuck out. My ex was the exact opposite. By the time I got to Ant's face, he had removed his hood and gave me a sexy smirk.

"You fine, too, mama," he complimented, making me giggle.

"How can I help you, handsome?" Yes, I openly flirted with the fine specimen in front of me. For the first time in a long time, I didn't feel guilty about it.

"I need my dreads re-twisted. I'm looking for someone named Kris. I heard she was the best loctician in Harlem."

"That would be me and you heard right. Come have a seat, let me hook you up." He sat down, and I got prepared to do my thang.

As I serviced him, we flirted back and forth until I was done. Satisfied with the finished product, he paid and promised he'd be back when it was time to twist them again. He shocked me when he didn't ask for my number, but of course, I played it cool.

I didn't see him again until a few weeks later, and this time, he asked for my number. I shot him down, figuring I'd make him wait it out just like I waited for him to ask me. His persistence paid off because he ended up circumventing me and getting my number from Heaven. Imagine my surprise when he texted me out of nowhere, in the middle of the night. That night, we spoke until the sun came up and had been getting to know each other ever since. In that time, I learned that he had a brother and was the father of a four-year-old.

The ringing of my phone pulled me from my trip down memory lane. I smiled big when I saw the incoming Face-Time call from Ant. Quickly swiping right, his face came into view.

"**Hey, you,**" I answered, my face lighting up like a Christmas tree in December.

"**Wassup, ma? Tell me we on for next Friday night,**" he spoke in his cool voice. He was always so chill.

"**Yes, we're good to go. My sister is down for the double date as well so make sure you prep your brother about that mouth of his.**" He had let me know that his brother had no filter and always said what was on his mind, good or bad. That certainly wasn't going to work with Kaia. She would go off on his ass and dare him to buck at her.

"**I got him. He gon' be good. Besides, he knows how hard I've been working for you to give me a shot. I'll beat**

his ass if he fucks this up for me." I laughed at his threat, knowing I hadn't made it easy for him.

"Well, hopefully, it won't come to that. I gotta tell you, I'm actually looking forward to this date. It's been a while since I've been out with a guy." Admitting that out loud, I hoped I didn't come off as the female that was looking for a man. That most certainly was not the case. I'd gone on a couple dates after leaving Kane but none of them ever made it pass the dinner table.

"I'm looking forward to it, too, ma. Trust me, this will be your *last* date. But aye, I'm on my way to see Breann, I'm gonna hit you later. Pray for me, ma."

He always said that when he was going around his baby mother. From what I gathered, they didn't get along at all. I often thought if I did give him a chance, would I have to deal with that drama, too? I guess I'd see once we reached that point. We said our goodbyes and hung up as I parked in front of my shop.

I had been renting the space from a sweet older lady whose son was a barber and had passed away. She didn't know a thing about the hair business and when I saw the for-sale sign, I jumped right on it. I was just three payments away from owning the place. I felt so accomplished. Strolling up to the building, I used my key to open the doors. As soon as I walked in, the lights illuminated the place. I loved my shop. Currently I employed four stylists, including myself. Heaven,

Mia, Nay, and I may have been a small team, but our work spoke for itself.

We all were passionate about hair and were the best at what we did. I loved being the boss and took pride in my business, hence, the reason I was always here an hour before opening. I took inventory and made sure my staff had everything they needed to give the best customer experience. After ensuring everything was set up, I checked my appointments and ordered breakfast for the staff.

A knock at the window caused me to look up from where I stood at the receptionist desk. My body froze at the sight of Kane standing at the door with a handful of roses and a stupid smile. I didn't know I was shaking until the phone fell out of my hand. Quickly picking up the receiver, I placed it back on the cradle. On the outside Kane was so well put together. His handsome features made women flock to him.

He was of Dominican descent with gray eyes and a head full of soft, curly hair that you wanted to play in. He was physically fit and quite smart. Most of all, he was powerful. Kane was a good ol' boy in blue. Yes, a cop. For that reason alone, I suffered through years of abuse in silence and never reported him.

He liked that he had that power over me. I knew for a fact that if it wasn't for the badge he hid behind, I would've tried to kill him a long time ago. That and the fact that over the years, he'd programmed me to fear him. Another knock at the window, more aggressive than the first one made me jump.

"What do you want, Kane?" I broke my silence, speaking loud enough for him to hear. I had no intentions on moving from where I stood and hadn't even considered opening the door.

"Are we really gonna talk through the glass, Kristen? Come on, I come in peace. I swear." He lifted his free hand as if to signify some kind of promise.

"Any promise that you make holds no weight with me, Kane. Again, why are you here?"

"I came to apologize, baby. At least let me give you the roses," he pleaded.

"Leave them at the door and go about your business. As you can see, I'm doing well, and I don't *need* nor do I *want* your apologies. Too little, too late, and I'm good." The fucking nerve of this clown. I could see his jaw flex and his forehead crease. Two signs that indicated he was about to go left.

"I see you're still a stupid bitch. Here I am trying to right my wrongs and you're giving me a hard time. Open this fucking door, Kristen, before I break it!" His outburst made me pull out my cell phone and start recording while my other hand went to the desk phone to call 911.

"Stop, Kane! I'm gonna get yo' ass arrested... I'm not playing." The phone was in my hand and my finger rested on the number nine button.

"Fuck you, I *am* the law! You lucky I have somewhere to be, or I'd break this door down and break yo' face." Smacking the glass angrily, he spit on it. Throwing the flowers to the ground, he finally walked away.

I watched him get in his car, that was double parked next to mine and immediately called Heaven once he sped off. I knew it would only be a matter of time before he popped up. Kane was going to be a problem and I didn't want Ant involved in the fatal attraction I was dealing with. After explaining what happened to Heaven, she rushed over with her husband, Derek. I tried to protest when she said she was bringing him, but she wasn't having it. Kane had threatened me out in the open so I knew his behavior would only get worse.

Thirty minutes later, Heaven came busting through the salon door. "Where that motherfucka at?!" She yelled, barging through the shop.

"He left already, boo," I said, still standing in the same spot. She came over to hug me and stood back to check me out. After giving me a good look over, she continued her rant.

"Derek circled the block just to make sure his punk ass ain't lurking around. Ughh, he made this fucking mess and spit on the fucking glass. Oh, his mother definitely was on that shit when she was pregnant with him. This shit is crazy. You need to press charges on that motherfucka."

"Just so he can find a way to get in the system and make

them disappear, no thanks. I'd rather not waste my time." I waved her off.

"So, what we gon' do then? Wait until you're laid up in the hospital again, Kristen?" *Damn, that was a low blow.* I'm guessing she thought so, too, because she apologized and hugged me again. "You know I'd lose my mind if something like that was to happen again. I didn't have to say that, though." She was so sincere, I couldn't help but to tear up. I didn't want anything to happen to me either.

"You good. I circled the block twice and didn't see his car," Derek reported as he entered the shop. "You call when you need me, cuz. We family, and I got you," he assured me. He was more like a big brother than a cousin. He and Heaven had been together since high school. After thanking him for coming out, he kissed Heaven and left for work.

Taking a moment to get myself together, I had Heaven clean up the flowers and trash them while I wiped Kane's spit off the window. By the time I regrouped, the other stylists had arrived. I put on my perfect smile and the rest of the day continued without incident. At closing time, Heaven opted to stay behind with me to do some last-minute tidying up and count the day's profits. My phone chimed in my smock, making my brain pause so I wouldn't lose count. Pulling out the phone, there was a text from Ant.

Crush: *Shorty, I had a rough day. Let me pull up on you real quick. I need to see your face.*

Me: 🙁 *you and me both, and yes, you can stop by. I'm just shutting everything down at the shop for the night.*

"Okay, boo, I'm outta here. You need a ride home?"

"No, I'm good. Ant should be here in a few." I didn't notice the change in my demeanor when I mentioned his name, but Heaven picked up on it quick.

"Oooh, that's yo' man now, huh? The way your shoulders touched your ears and that smile at the mere mention of his name said *everything*. Yess, boo, you betta go get yo' happiness." Her dramatic ass started dancing in the mirror.

"Bye, Heaven. Ain't yo' husband outside waiting on you?" I laughed and shooed her.

"Bye my ass, I'm staying till he walks in. Let me text Derek and let him know. Shit, *crazy* might try to roll up in here and we'd have to jump his ass." I just shook my head and grilled her. "Too soon?"

"Yes, heffa." I laughed again at the apologetic expression on her face. Not even ten minutes later, Ant showed up at the door with McDonald's bags in his hand. Walking to the door to let him in, I chuckled when he held the bags up to me like they held a five-star meal.

"Aww, you're so sweet. You didn't have to do this," I gushed, kissing his cheek.

"Girl, that is not sweet, that's cheap as hell. I know you getting to a bag, Ant, don't play with my cousin."

He smirked and told Heaven to count her husband's

pockets and not his. We hugged again and she went to leave, but not before threatening Ant to make sure I was safe.

"I wouldn't let a soul disturb a hair on her pretty little head." His statement made me blush and Heaven put her finger in her mouth like she was throwing up.

"Nigga, you ain't smooth. Goodnight, love birds in training." Throwing up the peace sign, she made her exit.

"Yo' cousin is a trip."

"This I know. I couldn't see life without her, though."

We sat across from each other at the stylist booth and he handed me my bag. I looked at him with a raised brow, wondering why it was so heavy. He gave me a nod to open it. I fell out laughing as I pulled out the contents of the bag and placed them on my station.

"McDonald's, Chipotle, Taco Bell, and Popeyes. Really, Antwon? Where I'ma put all this food?"

"Shit, in yo' belly. A nigga on a budget, I can't afford to be wasteful." He smirked before opening his bag and pulling out the same food. He was a straight up comedian. Deciding to go with the Popeyes, I dug in like I hadn't eaten in two days. I skipped breakfast earlier after everything that happened with Kane's psychotic ass. "You ain't afraid to put yo' food away in front of yo' nigga, I like that."

Batting my eyes, I took a sip of my soda. "Who said you was my nigga?"

Ant

I had a comeback for Kris's question, but I was mesmerized by how beautiful she was. Although her beauty was unmatched, behind her big dough eyes held a story that I was ready to hear about whenever she was ready to tell me.

"I became *yo' nigga* soon as you gave me the green light for our date." She just smiled and didn't debate me.

"Heard you. Tell me about this rough day you had."

"Man, you know I have the baby mama from hell, right?"

Again, she smirked. "So, you say."

"Nah, ma, this shit is *real*. I really believe she was brought up from hell and planted on earth to aggravate a nigga."

Thinking I was joking, Kristen was getting a kick out of my misfortune.

"Okay, I'm sorry," she continued giggling. "Your face is priceless right now. Okay, go head, continue."

"Nah, you doing me wrong, shorty." I continued eating my food.

"Aww, you big baby." Getting up from her seat, she came over to me and wrapped her arms around my neck from behind.

"Damn, you smell good. What you got on?" Placing my food on the counter, I spun around in the chair to face her.

"If I tell you, you gon' have to buy me some more."

"Bet."

"It's YSL Libre."

"Cool." I stored the name in my mental rolodex. "You already know all about my problems. Tell me what happened with you today." She immediately cast her eyes to the ground, which let me know it was something she didn't want to talk about. "Not looking someone in their eyes when they're talking to you is usually a sign that you on some bull-shit, and even worse, a sign of deceit. So, either you bout to lie or you on some bullshit. Which one is it?" Lifting her head, her eyes bore into mine like she was tryna prove something.

"There's not a deceitful bone in my body." She spoke with so much conviction, it made my dick hard. "If I don't tell you something, it's for a reason." We had a stare down for a while before a ringing phone broke our concentration. She tilted her head to the side like it was someone calling me.

"Ion know why you lookin' at me, my phone damn sure ain't got no Rihanna ringtone." She chuckled before walking away. Discarding what was left of my food, I cleared off the station, making sure there was no mess.

"Sorry about that," she said, walking back over to me. "I gotta get home. My sister is using me as her alibi tonight."

"You good, ma. Make sure you hit me when you get there. Matter fact, grab ya bag, I'ma walk you to your car." I waited for her at the door while she did as I asked.

After ensuring she got to her car safely, I hopped in my Bentley Mulsanne and headed in the direction of the studio to meet up with my brother, Maine. My brother was my best friend. Three years my junior, we were more than close. Growing up with a single mom, I was pretty much the only father figure he'd ever known. It had always been us and my mom for as long as I could remember.

She may have been single and raising two hardheaded ass boys in the projects, but she always made sure we had. By hook or crook, Ma Jane, as the hood called her, was gon' get it out the mud. I couldn't tell you how many times she made a way out of no way. That woman raised great men and for that, I'd put my life on the line twice for her. Stopping at a red light, I picked up my phone to call my baby girl to say goodnight before she went to bed.

At four years old, my little girl had my heart in the palm

of her hand and she didn't even know it. She looked just like me and even had my mannerisms. The shit was crazy. I knew she wasn't up this late, but this was my ritual. I'd have her mother put the phone to her ear and I'd wish her a goodnight.

Hearing the phone connect after three rings, I spoke. **"Yo', can you put the phone to Bre's ear for me please?"** This was as nice as it got with Chloe.

"Hold up, blood, this ain't Chloe. Gimmie a minute, let me get her for you." Hearing a nigga's voice on the other end of the phone, I blew.

"Yo', who the fuck is this?!" I could hear shuffling in the background before Chloe's voice came through. I now had the call on speakerphone and sitting in the center console. I had to pull my car over on the side of the road to get my mind right.

"Wassup, Ant, what you need?" She answered, nonchalantly. Too nonchalant for me.

I took a deep breath before responding. **"You got a nigga in the house where my daughter rests her head?"**

"Oh boy, here we go. Look, that's my man, Jarrod. Don't even trip, he's been around Breann before." The fact that she let that shit role off her tongue so effortlessly and didn't see a problem with it further enraged me.

"Chloe, are you stupid or just dumb? Fuck you mean this nigga been around my child and I ain't even meet this man? You know I don't play that shit!" I roared into the phone. She was begging for me to push her shit back and leave my daughter motherless. She was lucky Bre loved her as much as she did, and I wasn't heartless.

"Fuck outta here, Ant, I don't answer to you. This is *my* shit. I can have whoever the fuck I want in here. You got me fucked up and confused with one of those bitches who move yo' dope for you."

"Bet." I hung up in her face soon as she started talking that Fed talk. Starting my car again, I made a U-turn and headed towards her crib. Dialing my brother, I told him to meet me there. **"And call mama, let her know she's gonna have some company tonight."**

"Got you." He hung up with no questions asked.

Maine knew whenever I called for him to link at Chloe's, it was bullshit involved. Pulling up to her apartment building in White Plains, I parked my car and got out, ready to disturb the peace. She didn't know that I had made a key for cases such as this. There were too many missing and abused kids on the news daily at the hands of parents' boyfriends or girlfriends. I was taking every necessary precaution to make sure my daughter wasn't the next story. Opening the door, I could hear music coming from Chloe's bedroom as I passed it and headed straight to Bre's. My baby girl could literally sleep through anything, so while I got her dressed, her eyes were still closed.

"Ant, what the fuck? I almost shot your stupid ass," Chloe whispered harshly as I stood up with Bre in my arms. She had the .380 Magnum I'd bought her when she first moved into the apartment pointed at me.

"Man, put that shit away and move so I can get my daughter up outta here. Yo ass wasn't that concerned. You got ya door closed, with the music on and shit. I could've been anybody walking up in here. And for the record, ya man is **a pussy**," I spat out loud, hoping he would hear me. "I know the both of you heard someone come in and *you* the one in here with a gun. You fuckin' wit a bitch ass nigga that's prolly in there hidin' and shit." Sucking my teeth, I walked around her.

"You not taking my daughter nowhere this late at night, Antwon." She went to walk in front of me, to block my path to the door, but the face I gave her made her think twice.

"Buck if you want to. You know I won't put my hands on a woman, but I'll have my mama over here in fifteen minutes. And you know you don't want those problems." She thought twice, allowed me to sidestep her, and I headed back out to the front. I opened the door and Maine was on the other side of it, about to knock.

"Oh, uhn uhn, why yo' brother here? You really overstepping your boundaries, Antwon. This shit not even cool." She knew Maine couldn't stand her and he didn't try to hide it either. I ignored her and handed Bre over to him as she started to stir.

"Bro, take her to the car. I'll be down in a minute." He nodded and went to walk away.

"Maine, stop fucking playing with me. Bring my child back here before I call the boys on y'all ass." Unlike myself, my brother was a loose cannon when provoked. It wasn't no saving Chloe from his wrath. We didn't play with the police. Turning around, he covered Bre's ear before speaking.

"Look, bitch, I came over here on some peaceful shit, but you know how I can get. I'm not Ant, I'll Donkey Kong yo' ass right on top of that water jug ass head of yours. Don't fucking threaten me." His eyes were menacing, and she knew if he said it, he meant it, so she left well enough alone. I shook my head at her as he walked away.

"I'm taking my daughter so you can entertain your company, but listen to me and listen to me good..." I pulled her by the back of her neck, not hard enough to hurt her, but enough for her to know I meant business. "You know I don't do well with threats, so think about what you say before you say it." Releasing her, she stumbled backward, dramatically. Her door opened and out came a scrawny nigga, in his boxers, with a blunt in his mouth. I bit the inside of my lip, knowing I was about to go ham out this bitch.

"You good, boo?" He asked Chloe who just hung her head. I could tell she was embarrassed.

"Nigga, you do know that a fucking four-year-old child lives here, too, right? Go put some fucking clothes on. Ya new niggas is weird as fuck."

"Man, fuck you, this..." I didn't let him finish before my right hook met his left eye.

"Antwon!" Chloe yelled my name just as he hit the ground and I lifted my leg to stomp his ass. "Antwon, go, just go."

Deciding his bum ass wasn't worth getting locked up for, I lowered my foot and left the building. This was the stupid shit I had to deal with because I nutted in the wrong woman.

Believe it or not, when I first met Chloe, it was *her brains* that attracted me to her. I ran into her a couple years back when I was going to check in with my lawyer on a bullshit case I picked up. She worked as a paralegal at the firm at that time. We sparked up a conversation and I was feeling her immediately. Fast forward a year into us talking, she got pregnant with Breann. She became a totally different person then. All she did was nag and complain about dumb shit. That was enough to get me to leave her ass alone.

She tried to control my relationship that I had with my daughter in the beginning, but I quickly shut that shit down. She learned quickly how I was coming behind Breann Rose Brown. The best thing I could've done for my sanity was let Chloe go. Making it back to my car, I got in the driver's seat while Maine sat in the passenger.

"Yo', ya bm is a fucking nut case."

"Who you telling, nigga? *I'm* the one that gotta deal with her for the next eighteen years."

"You a better man than me. I would've been a single father a long time ago." I knew what he was hinting at without him having to spell it out for me.

"Yeah, I know how you do. Good looking on coming out here, though. I'm about to head to mama's house and crash there for tonight." I looked back at my princess and grabbed at the little Ugg boots on her feet.

"You already know. Tell mama I'll be there in the morning for breakfast." He went to open the door and I remembered I had to remind him about the date.

"Yo' bro, don't forget about that double date next Friday. I'm counting on you, man," I expressed. He knew how important this was for me. I was really feeling Kristen.

"How can I forget? You mention that shit every day. I'm out here on the grind tryna finish this mixtape and feed these streets, I ain't got time to be making no love connection." It was just like him to dismiss the idea of possibly sparking a connection with anyone. His focus was his money and music. Women flocked to him, but I'd yet to see a girl around past two days.

"Bro, I need you on this one. You need to meet your future sister-in-law anyway." He raised a brow and I smirked.

"Aight man, whatever. I'll be there," he complied, clearly unhappy with the decision. Getting out of my car, he slammed the door.

"If Bre wasn't in this car I'd get out and beat yo' ass. Fake Dave East looking ass bitch." He laughed and gave me the finger before getting in his car and driving off. Once he pulled off, I did the same, en route to my mama's house. She lived twenty minutes from Chloe. I knew she was gonna be pissed about me having her grand baby out so late.

"Daddy," my princess called out to me. In the rearview mirror, I could see she was starting to wake up. She rubbed her eyes and squirmed in her car seat.

"Yes, princess?"

"Where I'm at?" She asked, making me laugh. This kid of mine was too much.

"You in my car, mamas. We going to grandma's house."

"Okay daddy, I tired."

Before I could respond, she'd knocked back out. I pulled into my mother's driveway and the security lights lit up. I made sure her security system was top of the line. In my line of business niggas were cutthroat. I knew it because I was one of those niggas who would lamp on you for weeks before you ever seen me coming.

You could never be too careful. And even though nobody wanted smoke with Ma Jane, I veered on the side of caution at all times. Picking Bre up, I kissed her forehead and fished my keys out of my pocket. Before I could get my key in the door good, my mother snatched it open.

"Gimmie my damn grand baby," she whispered harshly, to avoid waking Bre.

Removing her from my arms, she went to the back of the house, leaving me shaking my head. Closing the door behind me, I took my shoes off and placed them neatly on the shoe rack, in the foyer. I knew I wouldn't be going to sleep anytime soon, so I went to the living room and got comfortable on the couch.

"Uhn, uhn, getcho ass up. You not 'bout to sleep on my damn couch. You know I don't play that shit. Now that I got my grand baby down, tell me why you got her outside at this time of night like you done lost yo' damn mind." She went off just like I knew she would. She stood in front of me with her hand on her hip and a bonnet hanging off the side of her head, waiting for an explanation. I gave her the short version of what happened with Chloe, trying my best not to get mad all over again. "Chloe gon' make me go see about her, real talk."

"I told her that if she keeps doing dumb shit, I'ma take her ass to court for full custody." I was tired of going back and forth with Chloe. It was unnecessary because I gave her what she asked for when it came to Bre plus more. I didn't know what else the crazy bitch wanted.

"Let me have a conversation with her before you go that route. Remember, she is still Bre's mother and although she may not make the best decisions, she's a good mother. You need to get yo' business in order, too, before you start talking about custody," she reminded me without saying much.

I knew she was referring to my street dealings. She was right about that. To my family, I was Antwon or Ant for short. To these streets, I was "Ant the Dope man." Though I wasn't fond of the title these days, it was something I was good at.

I had mastered the art of cooking and moving big weight.

It was my thing, until I discovered my love and skill for scouting new talent in music. I had to thank my brother for that. Maine did this rap shit and you could say he was the first artist I discovered. I helped him hone-in on his craft and we had been going ever since. *Promise Records* was two years in the making and Maine was the star. I had plans to have this shit jumping by early next year.

"You right, and I'm working on that."

"You ain't gotta tell me, I'm always right. I'm headed to bed. Make this *the last* time you have my grand baby out this late or that's yo' ass." She mushed my head and went to walk away.

"Ain't nobody scared of you woman," I joked.

"You don't have to be scared, just be cautious. Period." I shook my head, knowing she had been listening to the City Girls again.

Maine

"Yo', run that back for me, Playboy," I called out to my engineer, who sat in front of a sound board while I laid down track after track in the booth. I didn't go home after leaving Ant. It was back to the studio for me. I heard my rhymes through the Beats by Dre headphones and closed my eyes as the words penetrated my ears. I made sure to put my life on wax every time I was in the booth. It was going on two in the morning by the time we finally wrapped the session.

This was my day to day. If I wasn't in the streets, I was in the studio. Single with no kids, the only people that meant anything to me was my moms, my brother, and my niece. I had no more room to love anyone else. Shit, I was too young to be thinking about that right now. I just wanted to stack my bread and make music. Not wanting to drive home, I decided to crash at the apartment I'd rented upstairs from the studio for late nights such as this.

It didn't take me long to get to sleep once I laid down. I'd been running all day and night; hell, my body welcomed the rest. It was around nine am the next morning when I awoke to my ringing phone.

"**Yooo,**" I answered without looking at the caller ID.

"**Don't yo' me. Get yo' black ass up and get to this house. I ain't cook all this damn food for nothing!**" My mom's voice came through loud enough for me to get my ass up like she said.

"**I'm up, Ma, I'm up.**"

"**Yeah, uh huh. Go wash yo' ass and I'll see you in a few.**" She hung up like she usually did when she was done talking. Sitting up, I said a quick prayer and got up to take a shower. I could've used some more sleep, but when my mama made a request, it was best you adhere to that shit. It took me all of thirty minutes to throw something simple on and head out the door.

Hopping in my Audi A7, I put the pedal to the metal to get there in a timely fashion. By the time I arrived, she and my brother were already at the table eating along with Bre.

She cut her eyes at me when I walked in with the smile that always got me out of trouble. Walking in her direction, I leaned down to hug and kiss her cheek.

"I'm not smiling witchu. I hope you wasn't doing anything last night with one of them lil' hoes, while you in here kissing on us," she snapped on me when I went to go kiss Bre.

"Ma, go 'head with all that." I grinned and went to wash my hands. "Wassup, bro?" I dapped him before taking a seat in the empty chair.

"Say grace, Tremaine." I frowned at her calling me by my full name. I still bowed my head, blessed the food, and got to eating.

"This good, Ma. Thank you for breakfast," Ant said while making sure Bre kept her food on the plate. She was going crazy on the Belgian waffles, scrambled eggs, and turkey bacon.

"No problem, baby. Y'all don't come see ya mama as often as I would like, so I cherish these moments here. Even though y'all get on my nerves at times." We laughed at her being sentimental. She'd never come out and say she missed us; she was too gangsta for that. My moms was the hardest out in my eyes. She played both mom and dad well. I don't know about Ant, but I didn't feel like I missed out on having a father figure at all.

"I'ma come around a lot more soon as I get this mixtape done, Ma. I promise."

"Me too, Ma. I found my future wife, so I'll be sure to bring her next time," Ant bragged with a smile, looking goofy as hell.

"Oh, yeah? Tell me more." Of course, she entertained him. I just continued to eat, minding my business. I didn't want any parts of the relationship conversation. "And what about you, Tremaine? You plan on slowing down soon or you still sticking that lil' thang in any girl with a coochie?" My niece laughed like she knew what her grandmother was talking about. I snickered at the advanced four-year-old.

"Ma, I don't stick my big thing into anything with a coochie," I corrected her. "I happen to have friends with benefits. I'll settle down when I'm ready and not a minute sooner."

"Mmhmm. Watch you find a woman that's gonna sweep you off yo' feet and get yo' ass right on together." She pointed at me, speaking matter factly.

"Maybe with Kristen's sister." I threw a piece of my waffle in Ant's direction. He knew what he was doing. My mother just shook her head at me. This nigga was such a dick head. I was glad she didn't ask him to elaborate.

"Aight, Ma, I'ma get up outta here. I love you." I hugged and kissed her and did the same to Bre who wiped my kiss off, making my mom laugh. I needed to hit the block. Every hustla knew, the early bird gets the worm. Ant walked me out and as soon as we got outside, I threw a jab at him that he ducked. "Why you tell Ma that shit about ol' girl?"

He laughed, knowing I was pissed off. "My bad, kid. It just slipped out."

"Nigga, you lyin' like a motherfucka. How this chick look, anyway? Since you promoting so damn hard. She got an Instagram?" I pulled out my phone and handed it to him, so he could show me her page. "She better be bad, too. I ain't being no wing man with no ugly chick, fuck the bullshit. I don't care what I agreed to."

"I don't have hers but here's Kris's. This is a picture of them together," he pointed out and handed me back the phone. "That's her on the left, bro. You know I ain't gon' hook you up with no butta face chick."

Checking her out, I tucked the phone back in my hoodie. "She aight." I tried to downplay it to him. Shorty was bad, though. Her face was void of any make-up, her eyes were bright, and her hair was pulled back from her face, in a pony-tail. Her smile was genuine, like she was really happy with life.

"Yeah, whateva nigga, you know she fine as hell. Just like her sister." I didn't answer, not giving him the satisfaction of knowing what was on my mind. Dapping him up, I got into my car and sped off.

Parking across from Drew Hamilton projects, I watched the block as the runners moved product like clockwork. Transactions were to be done in under a minute or niggas were getting docked. After sitting in my car for twenty minutes, I decided to make my presence known. Stepping out of my car, I casually walked across the street. Giving the runners a head nod, I casually walked into the building.

I didn't need to make a lot of noise when I was on the scene, niggas knew who I was. Standing at an even six feet, I couldn't be missed. Skipping the ride on the pissy elevator, I took the steps to the fifth-floor apartment that housed the work for this block. Knocking on the door, no one came immediately. Knocking again, only harder this time, somebody finally found some sense and answered.

"Yo', who the fuck is it?" The man on the other end barked. I didn't bother answering, just continued to count in my head how long I had been standing on the other side of the door. "I said who the fuck..." he paused once the door opened and he recognized me. "Oh shit, my fault, Maine." Dino held his hand to his chest apologetically. Now pissed, I hooked off on him, making him stumble. What bugged the fuck outta me was that nobody came to the front after hearing our conversation.

"Fuck y'all got going on in here?" I asked, pushing Dino into the living room. "Y'all niggas in here real relaxed when there's money to be made. Clean these fucking pizza boxes up!" I kicked the boxes in frustration. Niggas chilling on the clock was a definite no no. I sat on one of the dining room chairs and supervised their clean-up efforts.

"My bad again, Maine. I ain't know it was you at the door," Dino apologized with his hand out to dap me up. I declined and gave him a head nod instead.

"You good, man. Let me get that bread, so I can get up outta here." He went to the back of the apartment and returned seconds later with a Nike duffle bag. Thanking him for his assistance, I gave instructions for how I wanted shit to be moving when I came out the next time. Heading to my next destination, I went to collect from a few other traps before I ended up at the money spot to drop off the pick-ups. Securing the bags, I left to go to my own apartment.

I lived in a penthouse, nestled in the heart of Queens. My place was peaceful and serene. Before I could make it in my place, my phone rang for the first time today. Looking at the caller ID, I saw the name *Kandice*. Kandice was a little freak I'd met a couple months back at a party I passed through. She was cool peoples for the most part. She didn't want too much other than sex, at least that's what she claimed. That's what they all claimed until they saw it was the exact time I was on.

"**Wassup, shorty?**" I answered.

"**Hey, stranger, what you up to?**" I don't know how much of a stranger I could be seeing as I'd only fucked with her a couple times, but I went with it.

"**Nothing much, just got in the crib. About to whip up something for lunch and take a quick nap before heading to the studio later.**"

"Oh okay, you want some company?" The offer sounded good but nobody was coming to my crib that wasn't officially mine.

"Nah, but we might can link later. I'll hit you with an addy and we can play it by ear, cool?"

There was a pause before she responded. **"Umm, yeah, that's not a problem. I'll talk to you later."** She disconnected the call abruptly, which didn't make me no never mind.

Kicking my sneakers off at the door, I hung my keys on the key holder and made my way to the kitchen. As a single man, you'd think my fridge and cabinets would be empty, but it was quite the opposite. My moms made sure both mine and Ant's cribs stayed stocked with all types of shit, liquor included. Putting together a honey turkey and cheese sandwich, I finished it in under five minutes and washed it down with a bottle of alkaline water.

My place had an open floor plan. Everything was in plain view and I liked it that way. The floor to ceiling windows gave me a glimpse of the city that was real playa. Deciding to crash in the living room, I used the remote to close the curtains. Once the room was dark, I laid down and was out in minutes. What felt like an hour nap really turned out to be four.

Damn, I gotta start getting some more sleep, I thought to myself. Checking my watch, I noticed it was going on seven o' clock. Pulling out my phone, I went to my Instagram and absentmindedly scrolled through my feed to see what nonsense people were up to. It seemed like that's all the app was used for nowadays. That and promoting yourself if you had a legit business.

Amongst the people on the feed, a picture of Kandice and her friends popped up. They were sitting on the front stoop of a building, smoking and drinking. Kandice had her tongue out and middle finger in the air. The caption read, "What bad bitches look like." I shook my head because wasn't anything bad about the two chicks sitting on each side of her except for their bodies. Them bitches was rough looking. Logging out of the app, I went to put my phone back down and it rang. Seeing a call from Playboy, I answered.

"What's good, Play?"

"Boyyy, this shit you laid down last night is some heat. I got my cousin Eazy down here, he's an A&R executive down at Big Dawg Records. He wanna know what you doing with this track." He was hype, confirming what I already knew— a nigga had skills. I didn't like that my shit was being played for someone from a different record company, though. Promise Records was home and where I'd remain.

"Good shit, you got me on speaker, bruh?"

"Yeah, let me take you off real quick."

"Nah, you good. Aye, Eazy, I appreciate a good ear, I ain't looking to sign to anyone, though. Me and my bro got our own shit going on, feel me."

"Respect, my nigga. You got a banger for the streets. Good luck with everything."

"'Preciate that. Aye Playboy, I'ma hit you when I'm on my way down there later." Hanging up with him, I hit Kandice and told her the address of the studio. I needed to get this nut off, and she was ready and willing to help.

"THIS IS a nice place you got here," Kandice complimented while looking around.

"Thank you. You can have a seat on the couch. You want anything to drink?" I headed to the kitchen to grab a water.

"No, but let me taste you, though." I turned and she was standing behind me, ass naked. Moving closer, she dropped to her knees and pulled my pants down, releasing my dick. I gave her that, *what you 'bout to do with that* look. Her smirked before taking me into her mouth. "Mmm," moaning with her eyes closed, she ate the dick up like she had a point to prove.

"Uhh fuck, do that shit, girl." I grabbed her head and fucked her face, making her gag. She held on like a champion, too. I had never cum from head and although her shit was good, I knew it wasn't gon' happen today. She just kept on sucking, and I enjoyed it.

"Damn, are you ever gonna cum? My jaw about to lock up down here." I looked down at her with my dick in her hand and a wet mouth. I couldn't help but to bust out laughing. "That shit is not funny." She stood up with her arms folded.

"My bad, shorty. Come on, let me get up in that wet wet real quick."

Smiling, she turned around, and bent over the counter, assuming the position. Grabbing a rubber from my pocket, I slid it on, then slid into her. Her pussy was a little tighter than the last time. I think she used my advice when I told her she needed to start doing some Kegels and shit. Or google something to get that thang tight again.

"Mmm, yes daddy, fuck me," she voiced her appreciation for this LONG DICK. She tried to keep up with me by throwing her ass back, but when I grabbed a hold of her shoulder, I fucked all that competition right up outta her. "Ohh shit, Maine, I'm cummin'." I smacked her ass hard, leaving a red mark, and felt her pussy wet my dick up.

"Nah, we ain't done yet. Let me show you what this pussy can do." Lifting her leg up, I hit the pussy at an angle, making sure to tap her g-spot each time.

"Ouuu, this...feels...so...good," she let out, breathlessly. "I'm so wet."

"Throw that shit back. Come on, K." Leaning forward, she lay her head flat on the counter and bounced up and down. "That's right, get that dick." Feeling my nut build up, I pulled out of her and let loose in the condom.

"Damn, that was too good."

Making my way to the bathroom, I flushed the condom, cleaned my dick off, and tucked it back in my pants. When I came back out, she was already getting dressed. *You see what I mean?* Down with the program.

Kaia

Today was graduation day and I was on cloud nine. At the last minute, Heaven decided to try something new with my hair and added a few clip ins to make it fuller. It gave my tresses that extra bounce and body. Throwing on a floral Gucci romper and gladiator sandals, I was ready to fuck it up. And yes, T.I. put us on that Gucci ban, but this wasn't new Gucci. I had never worn this fit, and the g's weren't visible, so I got a pass. Kris had done my makeup, giving me a natural beat, you couldn't tell me I wasn't that girl.

"Mommy, don't start crying." I watched my mom as she failed at her attempt to stop her tears by fanning her face.

"Girl, ain't nobody crying, you know my allergies be acting up." Mase laughed at her while handing me a box from Tiffany&Co.

"Aww, thank you, Pops." I opened the box to find a diamond studded choker with my name on it.

"Now whose crying?" My mom teased as I teared up. Giggling, I stood up to hug him. The choker was bad than a motherfucka. "Here, let me put it on you." She took it from me and put it on my neck.

"Thank you for allowing me to be your Pops and being a great daughter. You and Kristen are the best things I have next to ya moms. I know I tell you all the time, but I'll tell you every day that I am so proud of you." He hugged me tight, and it felt good to know that my parents were proud.

"Wow, y'all couldn't wait for me to have a Kumbaya moment?" Kris pouted, standing in my doorway.

I waved her over and we all embraced each other before heading out. The graduation was held at a hall on 110th and Broadway. As we lined up in the hallway of the auditorium, I took a moment to calmly reflect over the last four years of school. I had more ups than downs, but it sure was a rollercoaster. College was the next step of course, but after countless talks, I was able persuade my mom and Mase in to agreeing to let me have my gap year. I planned to work on my sketches, and possibly shop my designs to a few fashion houses.

The standard graduation music played and one by one,

my fellow graduates and I walked to our seats. You could hear a bunch of awws throughout the auditorium and cameras flashing. We sat through what seemed like a thousand speakers before we finally got to the part that meant something to the students, walking across the stage. Once my name was called, my family as well as Shanice and Mecca stood to cheer me on. I took a page out of the Kappa's book and did that little shimmy with my shoulders after accepting the diploma. The students went crazy.

At the end, our principal announced our graduating class and instructed us to move our tassels to the right. We were the graduating class of 2020 and I did that shit. It was something about moving that tassel to the right that sent a surge through my body.

"We did it, bitches! Aye buss down graduiana," Mecca sang, and Kris joined in with us while our parents looked on.

"This the girl right here, Kandice?" A husky, hard faced lady walked up on us with Kandice next to her, mirroring her mug.

"Yeah, Ma," she confirmed. I didn't know what was going on, but I immediately pulled off my cap and gown and my girls followed suit.

"Excuse me, what's the issue?" The professional side of my mom spoke first. Meanwhile, both Mecca's and Shanice's moms were taking off their earrings.

"What's going on is *that* little bitch right behind you said she was gon' whip my daughter's ass after graduation. Well, here we are."

"First, let's tone it down with *the bitch* word. I'm sure if she said it, she meant it. We come from a line of women who say what they mean. However, this is a day of celebration and I'm sure if they fight right here, right now, I can promise you it won't be pretty. See, if one fight, baby, we all fight. So y'all go head and enjoy your day and we'll catch you at another time." Giving the duo her back, my mom locked her arms with mine and we dispersed with no further words spoken. I was sure I'd be seeing Kandice sooner than later.

Brushing the altercation off, we made our way to Kris's shop. She was throwing a little graduation party for me and the girls. It was supposed to be a surprise, but she couldn't hold water and ended up telling me this morning. Entering the shop, I gasped at how beautifully the place was decorated. It didn't look like a beauty shop but rather an event space. My sister had really gone all out for us.

"Thank you, sissy. This is so nice." I hugged her tightly.

"Yeahhh, Kris, you did the damn thing, boo," Mecca added, giving a hug of her own along with Shanice. We ate and celebrated our day with our parents. Our futures were bright, and we were well on our way to success from here.

"STOP DRAGGING YOUR FEET, Kaia, you already agreed to go," Kris fussed at me as I walked slowly to the shower to get ready for this stupid double date.

I had a change of heart at the last minute, but I couldn't back out on her. I didn't have to be happy about it, though. After a good shower, I got dressed in a pair of Joe jeans and a body suit from the Shane Justin collection. Throwing on my Dsquared sneakers, I leaned against her room door with my arms folded.

"You rushing me and yo' ass still sitting in the mirror, in yo' bra."

"All I gotta do is slip on my shirt and sneakers. Fix yo' face, it's not gonna be bad."

"Whatever." Sucking my teeth, I went to the livingroom and plopped down on the couch. Taking out my phone, I went straight to my group chat. Opening the text thread, I typed.

Me: *I'm not tryna go on this damn date.*

Mecca: *Lol, girl if you don't stop pouting. I can see yo' lip touching yo' chin through the phone.*

Sha: *Lmao, Mecca you stupid. Kaia, just give it a chance, boo. Who knows, Maine may end up being yo' future baby daddy.*

Me: *Remind me again why I texted y'all? Y'all supposed to be on my side.*

Mecca: *We are bitch, you just being dramatic. Go on the damn date and tell us about it later.*

Sha: *Yeah, what she said.*

I didn't even bother responding. Hearing a knock at the door, I went to answer it. Looking through the peephole, there was a very pregnant lady on the other side, looking irritated. I, on the other hand, was puzzled.

Opening the door, I held it slightly ajar and greeted the woman. "Hey, how can I help you?"

"No, you can't. Is Kristen here?" She spoke boldly like she didn't just knock on my sister's door.

"First off, tone it down. Kris, come to this door before I sock this hoe!" I yelled but didn't move from my position at the door. I normally wasn't so aggressive, but I would meet a bitch right where she was with no problem.

"Who you gon' sock? China, what the fuck are you doing at my house?" Kris pushed me to the side after her discovery.

Now, I was on high alert. Based on her tone of voice she wasn't too happy to see the visitor.

"I'm here to tell you to stay away from Kane. We have a child on the way and we're a family." She rubbed her belly like somebody gave a fuck.

I checked my sister's reaction to see if the baby comment got to her. Seeing that she wasn't moved, I was proud. That meant she was officially over Kane's wack ass.

"Girl, tell yo' baby daddy to stay away from *me*. You popping up at my shit like you want a problem..."

"And I promise you don't," I interrupted before Kris continued.

"Girl, fuck you and that baby, fuck outta here!" Kris barked before slamming the door in China's face. "I'm almost done. Let me just grab my bag and put some lip gloss on." She walked away, leaving me stunned and proud. There was no need to expound on the situation. When she was ready to talk, we would.

CLYDE FRAZIER'S was packed with people. I was happy that Kris had Ant reserve seats for us downstairs beforehand. After giving the waitress the name our party was under, we headed in that direction. I had been to the restaurant a couple times, both with family and friends so I knew the menu like the back of my hand. When we got to the downstairs level, it was empty with the exception of Ant and Maine.

Hearing us walk over, Ant raised his head first and smiled. For the first time, I took notice of his nice ass teeth and the small diamond implanted in a tooth on the left side. He went to kiss Kris's cheek and it landed on the side of her mouth. She blushed hard and I knew I was in for a long night of watching my sister be coy with a boy.

"Nice to meet you, sis." He gave me a welcoming hug.

"Oh, we related?" I joked and he laughed.

"God willing." He gazed at my sister again. The whole time we interacted, Maine hadn't lifted his head not once to acknowledge us. And I had to deal with this asshole. "Bro, put ya phone down and great the ladies."

He put his head up briefly and spoke. "What's good," he said unenthused, and Ant shook his head.

Like a gentleman, Ant went to pull out our chairs for us to sit, only Maine's foot was in mine. I already didn't want to be on the date, so I definitely wasn't about to deal with his shit.

"Boy, move yo' damn foot." Smacking his leg, his foot fell. Changing the seat, I sat down. I could hear Ant and my sister chuckling, but I didn't find shit funny. A few minutes later, the waitress came over to take our order. I ordered the blackened butter salmon with bourbon butter, spinach, and potatoes. My mouth watered as I thought about one of my favorite meals on the menu.

"Yo', how that salmon taste?" Maine asked once the waitress walked away. I ignored his ass just as he'd done us when we walked in. His fine ass had me fucked up. He clearly had some kind of complex. "Shorty, you don't hear me talking to you?" He tapped my arm and I pulled it back.

"My name is Kaia, not shorty. Now you found ya voice?"

"What you mean? I spoke when you came in."

"If you consider, *what's good* speaking then you clearly weren't raised right." Rolling my eyes, I pulled out my phone and scrolled through Instagram.

My ignore game was strong. I wasn't going to interrupt Kris and Ant either. Our tables were separate for a reason.

The waitress came back twenty minutes later with our food. Maine had roasted chicken with garlic gravy over roasted potatoes. It looked good as hell, but I dared not to ask him to taste it.

"I'll give you a piece of my chicken if I can taste your salmon," he offered while eyeing my food. I wanted to say fuck him, but his food looked just as good as mine. I watched him cut a piece and he held his fork up to my mouth. I looked at him like he was crazy. "What? I don't have the cooties, ma."

"Hmph, but I'm sure you eat coochie. I'll use my own fork, thank you." I grabbed at the meat with my fork and put it in my mouth. "Mmmm, damn that's good as hell. Here." I took his fork and put a piece of salmon on it.

"You real slick for that comment. For your information, I don't eat pussy. I'm saving that activity for my girl. Feed me that." I don't know what it was, but I found his demand so sexy, so I complied. The way his jaw flexed as he chewed had me squirming in my seat.

"Sis, come with me to the bathroom real quick," Kris requested, snapping me out of the trance Maine had me in. Getting up, I followed behind her. "I see you over there making nice. Thank you for holding it down for me."

"I'm glad you know I'm only doing this for you. I could give a damn about his rude ass." I waited for her to use the bathroom and we both washed our hands once she was done.

"Mmhmm," she commented.

"Mmhmm nothing. Don't nobody want no Maine."

"So why you feed him some of your food? One of your favorite dishes might I add."

"Why you focusing on me when you on a date?" I was caught, but I wasn't admitting to nothing.

She shook her head. "Alright. I'ma let you have it tonight. We can talk about it later. Come on, I'm sure they're missing us." We left the bathroom, with me hoping that Maine didn't catch on to how he was making me feel the way my sister had.

Kristen

Kaia could act like she wasn't interested in Maine all she wanted, but I knew better. My sister didn't play when it came to food, money, or sleep, so when she gave him a piece of her salmon, I knew what was up. I was glad she didn't bail on me tonight. I really needed her presence, especially after China showed up to my door. I did good at masking my hurt in front if Kaia, but I really wanted to spazz out and cry. Not because I wanted Kane's crazy ass or the babies that I'd aborted each time I got pregnant. Yes, I had been pregnant a total of three times.

I was mad at the fact that I was right all along about their secret relationship. This man popped up at my place of business, threatening me when he got a whole damn family at home. Shaking off thoughts of my past, I walked back to the table where Ant sat waiting for me. He had me laughing and smiling throughout the night. I was surprised my jaw wasn't hurting.

"You good, ma? I thought you fell in the toilet for a minute," he joked, and I stuck my tongue out at him.

"No, I didn't, smart ass. I see you enjoyed your food." He had wiped his plate clean with his greedy ass.

He shrugged his shoulders, not the least bit offended. "I always eat all my food, bae." He winked at me, and I squeezed my legs together, catching the sexual undertone in his statement. "Yo' bro, let's go get this game crackin'. They think they got game," he said to his brother like Kaia and I weren't sitting in front of them.

"You ain't said nothing but a word. We didn't come in jeans and sneakers for nothing," Kaia said while slapping me five. They didn't know it yet, but they were about to find out.

"Oh, they big shit talkers," Maine egged on. "Bet a stack then."

"Each," Kaia and I said at the same time.

"Yeah, I know y'all got it, big spender." I tapped Ant's pockets and he smirked at me.

"I guess we're about to be two stacks richer, bruh." Maine's cocky ass laughed.

We decided to play to ten points. I wasn't tryna be in the restaurant sweating out my hair. And sweat marks on my white Fendi shirt was a hell no. Minutes into the game, the guys were up by two points and just like I predicted, they were getting cocky. As Ant played defense, he made sure to rub his dick up against my ass so I could fill his hard on.

"You think humping me is gonna get you a W?"

"Nah, I don't give a fuck about this game. I just wanna be close to you." He was so close, the hairs on my neck stood up.

I leaned back and whispered to him, "I would do that dick so good, daddy." Before he could react, I pushed him off of me and took the ball to the basket, making a point. Kaia laughed, knowing exactly what I was up to.

"Nigga, really? You all hyped up behind a whisper? Play, man!" Maine spat and I fell out laughing. Kaia nicely caught the pass I sent her way and made a basket too, tying us at nine points.

"Point game, nucca. Come on witcho mad ass," Kaia teased. I stood in front of Ant as she posted Maine up. He kept talking shit and she faked him, making him stumble a little bit. Again, she made the basket. "And that's game, baby. Fuck 'em up, sis."

We both danced in celebration and they dug into their pockets to hand us our winnings. Returning to our tables, we gloated while they pouted. Maine more than Ant.

"I gotta admit, shorty, y'all surprised me. Who taught y'all to ball like that?" Ant inquired, reaching for my hand across the table. I placed mine in his and I swear it felt like it was only us in the room.

"Our sperm donor was into sports heavy, so he taught us the game."

"That's wassup. Beauty, brains, and you know ya way around the court. What size is your ring finger, ma?"

"Shut up," I smiled coyly. The waitress returned to collect our plates and handed us the check. "Dutch?" I questioned Kaia who nodded in agreement. We both went in our bags and placed cash on the table for our food, drinks, and tip.

"Oh nah, y'all not about to play us like some lame ass niggas. What the fuck is Dutch anyway?" Maine argued, confused. Ant sat back, looking just as lost.

"It's when you go half on the check, normally when you're on a date. Which this is not by the way," Kaia clarified. I gave her a look that said, "chill," and she shrugged her shoulders with a smirk. Ant looked at us both like we were crazy.

"Well, we don't do Dutch, ma. Here you go." Ant handed us both back our cash. "Nice gesture, but Maine already offered to pay, right bro?" He glanced over at Maine who nodded.

"Yeah, I'ma cash app you, bruh."

"Nigga, cash app my ass. I'm still waiting on that dub you were supposed to send me for that ass whipping I served on that solitaire game last week."

Smirking, Maine handed the waitress his black card to pay. Once the bill was taken care of, the guys walked us to the car. Kaia gave Maine a handshake, which by his facial expression, shocked him. She didn't even stress the look he gave her when she got in the car. Promising to call Ant once we reached home, I drove off.

"That wasn't that bad, now was it?"

"Basketball was nice," Kaia replied, trying to downplay the night. I guess she still wanted me to believe she wasn't feeling Maine.

"Okay, Stink, I'ma let you have that." She rolled her eyes and looked out the window. I snickered at her petty ass.

When we arrived back at my apartment, Kane was standing at my door. Now that there wasn't a barrier in between us like it had been at the shop, I froze. With Kaia walking behind me, she ran into my back when I stopped.

"Damn, Kris," she fussed. "That shit hurt."

Hearing my name, Kane looked in our direction. "Just the person I wanted to see," he let out. Feeling the tension, Kaia grabbed my hand and proceeded to walk towards my door.

"I don't know why you're here, but you need to get the fuck on and leave my sister alone." Kaia was bold like that. She didn't care that Kane was the police.

"Kaia, I'm not tryna bring no harm to your sister. I just wanna talk to her."

"Oh, like the pregnant chick that came here earlier? Boy, get the fuck outta here."

"Kane, you need to leave my building right now and don't show up here again. For the umpteenth time, I don't want *anything* to do with you," I finally found my voice to speak.

"China came by here?" He asked, puzzled.

"China, Asia, Beijing, whatever the bitch's name is don't matter. You take yo' ass whereva she is and don't come back." Kaia used her key to open the door and I walked in first.

"Whatever she told you is a lie, Kristen!" He shouted before the door was slammed in his face.

Walking into my living room, I sat down on the couch. I hoped that Kane wouldn't make a scene like he had done last week. I lived in a nice high rise in Manhattan and I'd hate to be fined for his stupidity. Kaia sat next to me and I laid my head on her shoulder. This was one of the things that I loved about our bond.

When I felt weak physically or emotionally, she was my strength and vice versa. Now, I wasn't scared of Kane the person, I was scared of Kane the cop. And when I looked at him, I saw a boy in blue. He was as dirty as they came, and I knew for a fact that he was into some illegal shit.

"I got you, sis," Kaia assured me.

"Siempre." (Always)

THE NEXT DAY, I woke up in a better mood than when I had gone to sleep. Today, Kaia was scheduled to take her road test. She'd been begging me to take her and the scheduled testing time just happened to be right before I had to go into the shop. What she didn't know was that our parents would be meeting us there with her graduation present. I had to hold my excitement in, to keep from ruining the surprise.

Making her a quick breakfast of sausage, grits, and eggs, I poured her a glass of apple juice and took it to her room. Knocking, she gave me the okay to enter. Opening the door, I wasn't surprised to find her still in bed. Kaia was not a morning person at all.

"Rise and shine, graduate," I sang in a lively tone, pissing her off.

"Ughh, come on, give me a few more hours," she groaned with the covers over her head.

"Come on, Stink, I made you breakfast." That made her peek from under the blanket. I held the tray up to show the spread I had put together. She smiled and got up quickly. "Uhn, uhn, go slay that dragon," I said, referring to her morning breath. Giving me the finger, she walked across the hall to the bathroom, returning minutes later.

"Thank you, sissy." Picking up the tray, she put a spoon and a half of sugar in her grits, making me mad.

"No problem, boo. You so weird with that sugar shit. I could've just made you farina for all that."

"Aye, my food, my choice."

"Whatever. Don't go back to sleep, remember your driving test is in a few. I'm gonna take you, so be ready in an hour." Moving the tray, she hopped up and gave me a big hug and kisses on my cheek. "Alrighttt," I laughed. "Let me go get dressed."

Being that I took forever to get started, I needed to get a head start. Back in my room, I grabbed my robe for the shower. I went to walk out when I heard my phone ring. Picking it up from the nightstand, the caller ID read, *unknown*. Sliding the talk button across the screen, I answered.

"Hello."

"Kris, it's me." Recognizing Kane's voice, I hung up.

I had changed my number a total of three times because of him. Somehow, to my dismay, he always got the new number. Before I could put the phone down, it rang again. This time, it was the ringtone I'd assigned to Antwon.

I know we just chillin' but my body is on a mission, you know I flow witchu, did I forget to mention, your love is out this world, it's on another dimension. The lyrics to Summerella's "On a Mission" played, giving me goosebumps, anticipating talking to him.

"Yo', turn that shit down, I'm on the phone." I heard him bark at someone in the background.

"Umm, helloo," I let out so that he knew I had picked up.

"My bad ma, wassup?"

"Nothing much, getting ready to head out with my sister to take her driving test." Plugging my AirPods in my ear, I walked to the bathroom. It wouldn't be the first time I'd showered with him on the phone.

"Oh, aight. Tell her I said, good luck."

"Will do."

He paused before speaking again. "You think I can have a little of your time tonight?"

"Yeah, I think I can fit you in my schedule."

"Good. I miss your presence already."

I blushed, loving the fact that he spoke on how he truly felt. He didn't beat around the bush or try to act too smooth when it came to me.

"Aww, I miss you, too."

"That's good to know. I ain't gon' hold ya line, though. Have a good day, and we'll set something up for later."

"Sounds like a plan. You have a better day." I lingered on the line a little longer and all that could be heard was light talking in the background, on his end and water running on my end. "You gotta hang up."

"I know, I just don't want to yet. You in the shower?"

"Uh huh."

"I'll stay on till you get out. I wanna feel like I'm there."

I smiled and used my loofah to exfoliate. "Well, if you gonna be here, you gotta wash my back."

"Aight, gimmie the rag," he played along.

I stayed in the shower ten minutes longer than usual, with us hanging up after confirming plans for later again. Putting on my robe, I went to check on Kaia to make sure she was getting dressed.

"Don't be clocking me, I'm dressed already, boo," she said, standing in front of the mirror, slicking her hair into a ponytail.

"Okay, just making sure." Returning to my room, I threw on a pair of Palm Angels joggers and t-shirt, slid my feet into a pair of Ego shoes, and we headed out. Kaia didn't look nervous at all when we made it to the driver's ed place. In fact, she looked more than confident.

"Let me go in here and kill it," she said, stepping out of the car.

"Good luck!" I yelled out the window.

"Don't need it, I got this!" She boasted and gave me a thumbs up.

I parked across the street and sent my mother a text to let her know that we had arrived. She responded that she'd be by as soon as the test was done. I watched as Kaia got in the driver's ed car with her instructor and videotaped the car as she pulled off. The test took all of ten minutes.

When she turned the corner and pulled back onto the block, I stepped out of my car.

"So, what they say?" I questioned once she made it back to my car. The look on her face wasn't a good one.

"I passed!" She exclaimed, jumping into my arms.

I laughed hard, doing my best to hold her up. "You did itttt! I'm so proud of you, Stink!" The beeping of a horn halted our celebration, and I tapped her back, indicating for her to turn around. "Look."

"Oh, my Goddd, shut up y'all!" She froze at the sight of her new 2019 White Mercedes Benz C300 Coupe.

"We hear there's a newly licensed driver in need of a

whip," Mase said from the window of the driver's side. "Is that true?"

"Yes! Gimmie the keys!" Kaia rushed over to the driver side and snatched the door open. I was happy seeing my lil sis happy. Mission accomplished.

Ant

I sat in the studio, listening to Maine lay down the last track for his mixtape after getting off the phone with Kristen. Shorty was something special. I couldn't think of a time where I'd wanted a woman by my side so bad. Our double date was better than I expected, and I actually enjoyed her company. I already knew I owed bro for tagging along.

"Aight, come out so you can hear this," Playboy spoke to Maine.

He played the track back and I diverted my eyes to Maine with a smirk. The song was called "The One." I listened to the words and caught on to how he described Kristen's sister in detail.

"So, Kaia the one for you, huh, bro?"

"Huh?" He played dumb.

"Dawg, you just described Kaia on this song," I pointed out. He mentioned the date in the song and said her personality made her the one.

"Go 'head with that female shit." He waved me off. "This a regular ass song. A hit of course, but regular. Something the females can vibe to."

"Yo', whose Kaia?" Playboy asked.

Before I could answer, Maine beat me to it. "Someone whose off limits to you. Engineer, my nigga."

I laughed as he returned back to the booth. Yeah, he was feeling her. I'd fall back and let him admit it when he was ready. For the next few hours, I went over paperwork needed for us to get the building up and running for *Promise Records.* I was proud of myself being that much closer to removing both Maine and I from the game. My phone rung and the name *Pig* displayed. It was the new cop I'd just put on payroll a couple months back.

"Talk," I spoke into my AirPods.

"Wassup? It's me, Kane."

"Talk," I repeated. I wasn't on no friendly shit with police, whether they were on payroll or not. They provided information and I compensated them, simple as that.

"I just wanted you to know that one of ya young boys

got picked up earlier with a little weed on him. I'm cool with the officer that picked him up, so they didn't squeeze him too hard."

"Name?"

"Uhhh, Jhareel aka Lil' Rel."

"Copy. Make sure he gets home safe and let him know someone will be by to see him soon. I'll get witchu."

"Aight no..." I disconnected the call before he could continue.

After processing what I was told, I signaled to Maine to come out of the booth. Getting up from the couch, I walked out into the hallway, and he followed. I didn't want Playboy in our conversation.

"Yo', you gotta go check on Lil' Rel."

"For *what*? What happened?"

"Man, that lil' nigga got picked up by the boys and had some weed on him." Just saying it out loud had me tight.

"This lil' nigga gon' make me beat his ass. He shouldn't even be on the fucking block," Maine spat, angrily.

Lil' Rel was fourteen and Maine had taken him under his wing after finding him selling weed in the staircases of the projects he lived in. When Maine snatched him up, he said he was only making sales to get some money to feed himself and his seven-year-old sister. Their mother was a fein who barely stayed home long enough to ensure her kids were properly fed or even went to school. That's where Maine came in.

After hearing Rel's story, he gave him two hundred dollars, his personal cell number, and told him to stay his lil ass off the block. That was about six months ago, and Maine kept his word by looking after him and his sister. Shit was a sight to see, honestly. My brother had no patience, so him holding Lil' Rel down was admirable.

"Don't be too hard on him." I had a soft spot for the family.

"I'ma try, man. Lemme get outta here and pull up on his lil' ass now." He dapped me up and went to walk back into the studio.

"Aye, bro." He looked back to see what I wanted. "I'ma meet up with Kristen later. You want me to deliver a message to Kaia for you?" I tried to keep a straight face but failed and ended up smirking.

"Fuck you, Ant."

I bust out laughing. Packing up my paperwork, I headed to my mom's house to pick up Bre. I planned to take her back to her mother today. Chloe had been blowing my phone up for the past week about bringing Bre to her. She knew not to pop up at my crib or my mom's place especially. Although I was still pissed about the whole scene with her and her dude, I made sure to FaceTime her daily with Bre. I wasn't heartless.

"Ma, where you at?" I called out once I entered the house.

"We in the kitchen!" She yelled. Headed that way, I dropped my knapsack on the couch in the living room first. Entering the kitchen, I was shocked to see Chloe sitting at the island with Bre on her lap. I guess she was bolder than I thought.

"What you doing here?" I asked, choosing my words wisely. My mama didn't tolerate disrespect to women unless it was warranted. And she made the choice of *when* that was.

"I came to pick up my baby. Why you think I'm here?" I looked to my mom who crossed her arms and leaned against the sink.

"Don't look at me. She called and asked if she could come and get her child. I wasn't gonna tell her no. I texted you, too." I checked my phone and there was an unopened text from her that I'd missed.

"I don't know why she gotta explain. I mean, this is *my* child." Chloe twisted her neck as she spoke.

"Now slow ya roll, boo," my mom got to her before I could, and it was a good thing she did. I was ready to call Chloe out her name. "I *only* let you in here because you're her mother but make no mistake about it, I don't like yo' ass. Let me get my grand baby before y'all go." Chloe's jaw dropped. She left herself wide open for that. My mom left the kitchen with Bre in her arms, letting me kiss her cheek as she walked pass.

"You just love drama, don't you. I told you I was bringing her to you today, so why would you bring yo' ass up here?"

"Whateva, Ant. I couldn't trust that, so I came myself. I don't see what the problem is." I took a deep breath and decided against responding. Arguing with Chloe was like talking to a brick wall. "I heard you were at Clyde Fraziers last night with some chick." Her face was turned up and I laughed.

"Stay in yo' lane, Chloe. Oh, and make sure you keep yo' company out of yo' place when my daughter is there. You wanna pop that pussy, let me know and I'll pick her up."

"Oh, I can't have a friend, but you can be out on dates and shit? Kiss my ass, Ant, and go get my baby," she blacked, clearly pissed off. I did as she asked and went to get Bre from my mom. Handing her off, I helped load her in the car and kissed her forehead before Chloe peeled off.

"I really don't like that heffa. I can't deny that Bre lit up when she saw her, though," my mom griped as I walked back in the house, closing the door behind me. "Oh, tell me about the date y'all went on. Was ya brother acting an ass?" I laughed at her, knowing her baby boy so well.

"It was cool, Ma. Ya son is feeling Kaia. He even made a song about her." She looked at me with a raised brow before smiling.

"Well alright now. I knew there was hope for his mean ass."

"Yeah, Kaia wasn't having it. She actually had him smiling."

"Yeah, she's a winner." We both laughed, knowing what it took to get close to Tremaine. Kaia had managed to leave a lasting impression.

LATER IN THE EVENING, I met up with Kristen at her place. She decided she didn't want to go out at the last minute. That was cool with me. I even decided to cook for her. I mainly cooked for my daughter when she was with me, so I figured cooking for her would be easy. Parking across the street from her building, I grabbed the flowers I bought and made my way across the street.

I didn't think I'd be invited to the crib on my second date. A nigga was just that fly, I guess. Stepping onto the sidewalk in front of her building, the door swung open and the new cop on my payroll walked through it with a scowl on his face. I proceeded to walk pass him and he stopped me mid stride.

"Hey, Ant, wassup?" He held out his hand for me to shake and I looked at him like he was crazy. Embarrassed, he pulled his hand back and tucked it in his pocket. "What you doing out this way?" This nigga was either on the job or just nosey as hell. Either way, he needed to get the fuck on.

"You got something to report to me?"

"Report?" Confusion was written on his face, while my expression was that of annoyance.

"Yeah, report. I pay you to report shit to me, nothing more, nothing less."

"I hear you."

"Cool. You be safe in these streets, Detective." I entered the building, leaving him standing there.

Giving the doorman my name, he gave me the okay to head up. In the elevator, I leaned against the mirror. It felt like my lack of sleep was catching up to me. Between making sure that the streets were getting fed and going legit, I slept four hours tops on the daily. The elevator dinged on the 7th floor, and I stepped out. Going back to the text she sent earlier, I verified the apartment number before knocking on the door.

"Who is it?" She didn't have the normal smile in her voice that I'd become used to.

"It's me, Ant." The door opened and she looked like she'd been crying. "Wassup ma, why ya eyes red?"

She shied away from me in attempt to get herself together while I closed the door behind me. "Personal issues, I'm okay, though. Come on in the kitchen, I have all the ingredients for you to make my favorite meal, spaghetti." Grabbing me by the hand, she led the way. I wanted to press the issue, but like I said before, I wanted her to open up to me on her own. Rubbing my hands together, I surveyed the ingredients she'd laid out.

"Okay, I can work with this. Go sit yo' pretty ass down and let me do what I do."

"Well alright, chef. I'll be in the living room with my glass of wine. Try not to burn my house down," she clowned, leaving the kitchen.

It only took me thirty minutes to whip up the spaghetti and garlic bread. I sprinkled parmesan cheese on top and set the plates down on her dining room table.

"Ahh shit, it smells good in here. Let me see what you got going on." She looked at the spread on the table and smiled. "This is cute, boo. Now sit down so I can do the taste test. I'll grab drinks. Henny, Kool-Aid, soda, or water?"

"I'll take henny and Coke." Washing my hands again, I took a seat directly across from her. Reaching over, I took her hand in mine before praying over our food. When I lifted my head, she looked shocked and impressed. "What, ma? God loves thugs, too." She laughed and we dug in. During the meal, she moaned, and licked her lips, complimenting how good the food was. That shit had me rocked up, but I wouldn't tell her that.

"Oh my God, mmm, this is so good. What you put in here, Antwon?"

"Let's play a game. For each guess you get right, you get a kiss."

She sat her fork down and folded her arms. "Who said I wanted to kiss you?"

"You did when you just bit your bottom lip. Now go head

and start guessing." By the time she finished guessing, my lips were dry. She had guessed each ingredient correctly and was just missing one. "Aight, you got one more." Dipping my finger in the sauce, I held it to her lips. I smirked, thinking she was gonna smack my hand away. To my surprise, she moved closer, taking my finger into her mouth sensually.

Slowly sucking on it, she released me and sat back, grinning like a Chesire cat. "Sugar," she revealed. "The last ingredient is sugar."

"Damn girl, don't get that ass put in the air, sucking on my finger like that." Giggling, she winked at me and reached for my plate. Kristen was teasing and I was gonna play the game. I helped her load the dishwasher and we went into the living room.

"Come on, let's watch that series on Netflix, *When They See Us*. I've been wanting to watch it for some time now but haven't been able to bring myself to do it alone." Grabbing my drink, I sat down, and she got comfortable in my lap. "If you cry, I ain't gon' tell nobody, I promise."

"Woman please, ain't nobody crying over no movie." By the time we got to the end of the series, we both were wiping the corners of our eyes. "That's some bullshit, man. I remember the story but damn, I didn't know they carried them guys like that." The series had me heated. The men went through hell, especially Korey.

"I don't wanna talk about it. Here, let's play *2k*." She handed me a remote control from the side table and walked over to the tv to power on a PS4. I looked on in awe. I *knew* she was wifey material. We played for an hour straight and I won, of course. This time I wasn't fazed by her lustful stare and sexual innuendoes.

"Game, baby, who da man?" I stood up, relishing in my victory as she laughed.

"You got it. I ain't no hater. I'll give props where it's due." I reached out my hand and she gave me hers to shake on. Pulling her up from the couch, I caressed the small of her back. I was attracted to her sexually, but she also managed to stimulate my mind. That was a plus in my book.

"You're beautiful, you know that?"

She blushed under my stare and moved a piece of hair behind her ear.

"Thank you, handsome." I towered over her five-foot six frame at six foot one, so I reached down and kissed her lips. Opening her mouth, she slipped her tongue into mine. Caught up in the moment, I laid her down on the couch, and fondled her nipples through her shirt. "Wait, wait, Antwon."

Backing up off her, I put some space between us. "My bad, ma. I got caught up in the heat of the moment. I'ma get up outta here and head home." I went to stand up and she grabbed my hand.

"No, stay." Her voice held a longing for me in it, so I stayed.

Maine

Ever since that date with Kaia, I had been trying to fuck her out of my mind. I could admit I was being an asshole in the beginning, but the way she reacted sparked my interest. Other females I had come in contact with would have still been on my dick, even with me acting an ass. Not Kaia, though. And I hated to admit it, but I wanted her.

"So, you called me down here to zone out on me?" Kandice's voice brought me back after I'd drifted off. I had pulled up on her in hopes of clearing my head with some head before going to check up on Lil' Rel. This shit was Kaia's fault.

"Chill with the attitude, girl."

"I'm sorry, boo. You look stressed, let me help ease your mind." She reached over the center console of my car and wasted no time pulling my big man out my pants. Stroking him awake, she peered at me, eyes low, in an effort to be seductive. My face remained stoic.

"Look, shorty, I need you to eat this dick up. Save all that cute shit for another time." I gave her a little push and her lips engulfed my dick. Thinking about Kaia's sexy ass lips wrapped around my joint, I put my hand on the back of Kandice's head and thrusted into her mouth until I came. "Oh shittt!" I yelled out, shocking both myself and her. She sat back up with a smile like she had done something.

"You feeling better now?"

"Yeah, I'ma holla at you a little later." Her smile turned into a frown at the mention of me leaving. I never said I wanted to chill when I hit her up, so the last thing she should've been was mad.

"You always with the bullshit, I swear. Let me get the fuck up outta here." Waiting for both of her feet to touch the pavement, I sped off, en route to Drew projects.

I spotted Lil' Rel outside soon as I pulled up on the block. It looked like he was arguing with one of the corner boys while his mother stood next to him looking crazy. I didn't care for Linda at all. The bitch cared more about stuffing shit up her nose than her own damn kids. Walking over to where they stood, I pushed through the first layer of the crowd that had formed.

"Jhareel, take yo' lil' ass upstairs. I'm a grown ass woman and I can do what I want!" His mother shouted, yanking from the hold he had on her arm. Her clothes were falling halfway off her body and her hair was in a matted ponytail. I knew Rel was embarrassed.

"Man, don't sell that shit to my mama no more. Ant and Maine already talked to y'all about that shit," Rel argued. The emotion was evident in his voice like he wanted to cry, but he held it down like I had taught him.

"Get the fuck outta here, lil' nigga. I'll sell to who I wanna sell to, including yo' mama. What you gon' do about it?" The runner spat.

Getting a little closer, I was able to identify the insubordinate as Kareem. His lack of respect had been a topic of a couple meetings lately. I had given a direct order for *no one* to serve Linda, so why Kareem thought he was exempt from my direction was a mystery to me. Today, he'd have to tell me.

"Ay yo', my man." I made my presence known and the crowd dispersed.

"Wassup, Maine." His body language was different than it had been a few seconds ago with Rel.

"Let me talk to you over here for a second." I nodded to the side of the building. "Linda, go upstairs with Rel, I'll be up there in a minute." Rel hung his head because he knew I was coming to get on him and Linda moved like I requested.

She had all that talk for these lil' niggas but knew not to fuck with me.

"I'm on the clock, bro, is it important?" The nigga Kareem had the nerve to say. Somebody must've told Dino that I was on the block because he walked out the building.

"Yeah, nigga, it's my clock you on. Anytime, I ask to speak to you, deem it important."

"I'm sayin' though—."

"Nah," I cut him off. "I was tryna save you the embarrassment, but since you wanna do tough guy shit, go in the building, and give Dino whateva you have left. Your services are no longer needed." When I spoke it was law, so I didn't have to stick around to see if he did what I said. "If he jump stupid, make him feel it," I said to Dino as I walked pass. He nodded in understanding. Taking the steps to Rel's apartment, I could hear Linda yelling from the stairwell.

"You the reason that motherfucka is in our business in the first place. His yellow ass wanna come tell me how to raise my motherfuckin' kids, he don't know me!" I knew I was *the motherfucka* she was referring to. Knocking on the door, his little sister, Kelsey, answered.

"Hey, Maine," she spoke with sadness behind her voice. Kelsey was one of the smartest eight-year-old's I knew, and she was respectful. It was fucked up that she didn't have a role model in her mama.

"Hey, Kels. How you doing?"

"Umm, I'm okay, I guess. My stomach is on the gate and

mama spent the money you gave Rel last week for us. Other than that, I can't complain." Hearing that Linda's coke head ass spent the two hundred I gave Rel had me boiling.

"No worries, I got y'all. Go in your room and throw on one of the new outfits I got you. I'ma take y'all out to dinner." She hung her head when I said that. "What's wrong?"

"Mama sold those clothes, Maine. She said I don't need to be accepting nothing from grown ass men with my hot ass." Shaking my head, I pushed the door open and grabbed Kelsey's hand to follow me once I kicked it closed.

"Yo', what the fuck is yo' problem?" I spat, seeing Linda bent over the coffee table with a metro card, dividing up coke for use. Rel stood off in the corner with a disgusted look on his face.

"Maine, get the fuck outta my house! Kelsey, I'ma whip yo' ass for opening my damn door." She went to stand up but like an addict coming down off a high, her equilibrium was off, causing her to fall back down.

"Rel, take yo' sister and get ready. Y'all going with me." I spoke without even thinking. I just knew I needed to get these kids outta here. I didn't know the first thing about taking care of kids besides Bre and it was rare that Ant let me babysit. Rel moved quickly, not questioning where we were going. I knew he wanted to get the fuck up outta here. "Let me tell you something, bitch, those are some good kids in there and it's fucked up that they gotta deal with a sorry ass mother such as yourself. Until you get your shit together, don't come looking for them, aight? Matta fact, give me all their important paperwork."

"I got all our stuff, Maine, paperwork too," Rel spoke from behind me.

"Aight, leave those clothes, just take the papers. Take my keys and go get in the car." They walked out without thinking twice. I bent down close to Linda so that she could take heed to what I had to say next. "Somebody is gonna be by to visit you in twenty-four hours to take you to a rehab center for ninety days. You better go with them without a fight because they're going to call me if you don't. This shit ain't about you no more, it's about *those fucking kids!*" I stood back and she looked up at me with tear-filled eyes. I didn't know if it was from her high or if she was really crying. It didn't matter though because I meant what I said. "Twenty-four hours, Linda. Get this shit," I pointed to the coke, "out your system and be ready." With that, I walked out.

Getting in my car, I looked over at Rel in the passenger seat and Kelsey in my rearview mirror. Exhaustion was written all over their young faces. And not due to lack of sleep, but lack of *peace*. Reality had set in that I had taken this woman's kids, and I didn't know my next move beyond getting them fed and some clothes. I just knew that something drastic had to be done. This being in touch with my emotions shit was not for me. The first thing I had set out to do was get them some food.

"What y'all wanna eat?"

"Ooh ooh, Maine, can we go to BBQs on forty-second street pleaseeee?" Kelsey begged with her fingers crossed.

"Nah Maine, we don't wanna take you out ya way. We can get Chinese or something," Rel interrupted, shutting Kelsey down. She pouted with her arms crossed and I smiled.

"Y'all good, we can do BBQs."

Kelsey shouted, *yes* in the backseat, and Rel gave her a look that made her tone down her excitement. I was gonna talk to him about that.

THE RIDE to forty-second didn't take long and it wasn't packed when we got there. We were seated by a waitress, and I told them to order whatever they wanted on the menu. Rel gave Kelsey his phone and headphones to keep her occupied while we waited on the food.

"Yo', what happened with you getting booked man?"

He hung his head before answering. "Man, I was just standing outside when those bum ass cops rolled up, locking niggas up."

"Look me in my eyes when you speak. According to the cop, you had some weed on you. You back to selling that shit after we agreed you wasn't going to?" He shrugged his shoulders. "Nah don't shrug yo' shoulders, tell me something."

"Yo', I appreciate your help and shit, Maine, but I gotta deal with this shit with my mother day in and day out, bro. I take care of my sister, you know that. I gotta make sure we eat at all times. Most of the time, when you give us money, my mama finds the shit and spends it anyway. I gotta keep something on me at all times. This shit hard, so I do what I gotta do for us." He gestured between himself and Kelsey.

I couldn't say much to that. I couldn't even say that I understood where he came from because my mother was there and always made sure Ant and I had. Rel had basically taken on the father role to his little sister. I could respect him wanting to go out and make shit happen for the both of them, but I couldn't let him do it this way.

"I'ma set something up for you. A legit job, and y'all not going back to ya mama's house for a little bit. She got some work to do." He looked confused, but I knew he trusted me enough to go with the flow. The food came and I watched them eat. Pulling out my phone, I texted Ant to let him know I needed him to send our cousin Amina over to Linda's house in the morning to get her checked into the rehab center she had set up in Queens. It was an in-patient facility and just what Linda needed.

"Well, hey, I didn't know you had kids." My heart rate quickened, and I looked up to see Kaia standing over me with another female.

"I don't, Shorty. This my lil' man and his sister."

"Oh, hey y'all. She is such the little cutie." Kelsey blushed at her compliment while Rel licked his lips like he wanted to get his mack on.

"Stand down, lil' nigga," I said to him as Kaia's friend laughed and she smirked.

"Well, I was just coming by to say hey. Y'all have a good night." She didn't give me a chance to respond before she walked away. Shorty was a trip for real.

"That's you, Maine?"

"'Bout to be," I responded while still watching her walk away.

The next stop we made after BBQs was to get them a couple fits to hold them over for the rest of the week. School was out for summer recess, so I didn't have to worry about taking them in the morning. Instead of taking them to my house, we went to the apartment above the studio where they'd be staying. I went in and changed the sheets on the bed while Rel helped Kelsey get ready for bed.

"Thank you, Maine. I really appreciate what you doing for me and my sister. I need to work to ensure we're good though."

"We'll talk more about that. Right now, get you some rest. Don't leave here for nothing. Everything you need is here; the fridge is stocked as well. I'll be downstairs in the studio." Leaving the apartment, I went downstairs. Now I had to figure out how to be a guardian.

Kaia

"So, you still gon' act like you don't like that man?" Shanice said once we got in my car and pulled off.

"Mind yo' damn business." I blushed on the low. I had been trying to convince everyone around me that I wasn't feeling Maine like that, but I was failing miserably. Even though he'd gotten it together on the date, I still played the tough role. He wasn't just gon' say what he wanted to say to me.

"On the real though, Kaia, it's okay if you like him. I mean, I don't know him personally, but how bad could he be?"

"Girl, his fine ass is a menace."

"And those are yo kind of niggas, so what's your point?" I didn't respond because she was right.

We pulled up in front of Sephora to pick up Mecca from work and she was already standing outside waiting for us. I bust out laughing at the way she hopped in the car like fire was on her ass. "What the hell wrong witchu?"

"Bitch, my feet hurt from standing all day. I've been doing makeup since ten this morning. It is now going on eight in the evening. I almost sat my ass on the ground outside the store," she griped.

"Why you ain't just chill inside till we came?" Shanice asked.

"So, they could try to put me back to work? Hell nah, not happening." I continued laughing at her. For someone that hated their job so much, Mecca had not called out once and was always down for OT. "What we 'bout to do?"

"Well, I was thinking about heading to the studio to hang with this dude I've been kicking it with," Shanice answered, making Mecca and I look in her direction. "Why y'all looking at me like that? I told y'all about Playboy."

"She did?" I looked to Mecca for confirmation.

"Bitch, I don't know. You know I get high."

"Anyway, y'all wanna roll? We don't have to stay long, an hour tops, and it's in Harlem."

I shrugged my shoulders as she rattled off the address. I wasn't sure what to expect going to the studio, but the night was young and so were we. Arriving at the address, it was a brick building that looked decent, so I was a little less skeptical.

"This is it?" I verified with Shanice.

"Yeah. Let me call him and let him know I'm downstairs." I wasn't getting out until he gave her the okay. Meanwhile, Mecca was in the back, making sure she was put together.

"Bitch, it's a studio, who you think gon' be in there, Diddy?" I joked, cracking up.

"If it ain't him, I'll take one of the sons, ya hear me. Do them niggas like Lori Harvey real quick." She laughed with me and Shanice gave us the thumbs up to let us know were good. Getting out of the car, we walked up to the building and were immediately buzzed in. The outside of the building did the inside no justice. The marble floors were bomb and the fluorescent lights looked like they belonged in a building in downtown Manhattan, not the Eastside of Harlem.

"Glad you could make it, ma. I see you brought some company. How you ladies doing?" The guy I assumed was Playboy greeted us.

"We're good, thank you," Mecca answered for the both of us. He pulled Shanice in for a hug and they looked very familiar. I nudged Mecca and she gave me a look that said she caught on as well.

"Come on back. We were just in here vibin' to my home-boy's mixtape." We followed him and I'd be damned if it wasn't Maine sitting on a couch with his eyes closed, bobbing his head to the music. There was another guy at the mixing board smoking and bobbing his head as well. "Yo', we got company." Maine's eyes opened immediately and focused on me as if he could sense that I was in the room.

"And so we meet again," he said with a smirk.

"Oh, y'all know each other?" Playboy asked.

"Something like that," Maine responded, his eyes never leaving mine.

"Look, girl, I'ma need you to go entertain him while I go mingle with cutie at the mixing board," Mecca whispered in my ear. "Before you say no, remember all for one and one for all."

"Bitch, what does that even mean?" I countered.

"It means take one for the team, now go." She pushed me forward a little and Maine patted the seat next to him for me to sit down. I did, although I wasn't happy about it.

"Why you actin' like a nigga got something? You can sit back, ya know."

"I'm good just how I am, thank you." I sat up straight, not wanting to get too comfortable, in fear that I'd actually spark a conversation with him and like it.

"You mean as hell, you know that?"

"And you rude as hell, you know that?"

"So, I've been told, but I'm working on it." I did my best to try to hide the smile that was threatening to show on my face. He was tryna wear me down. A song came through the speakers, and the beat was so infectious, my head moved involuntarily. I knew it was Maine rapping just by the flow, but in listening to the words, it sounded like he was rapping about me. Both Shanice and Mecca looked in my direction but said nothing. The sly smiles on their faces said it all. "You like the song?"

"Is it about me?"

"What you think?"

"Don't answer a question with a question," I fired back, making him snicker.

"You just won't give me a break, shorty." I cut my eyes at him. "I mean, Kaia. What's wrong with that word?"

"It's common and ain't nothing about me common."

We stayed a little longer and ended up listening to his whole mixtape. I had relaxed a little bit, but not too much to make him think I was feeling him. I did enjoy watching him zone out to his music. Every now and then he'd close his eyes and lip sync the lyrics as if he was recording it for the first time. He wasn't the asshole I had met at the restaurant or this rude no-nonsense guy the hood talked about.

I liked *this* Maine. Checking my Apple watch, I noticed it was going on ten o'clock. Meaning, we had passed our hour limit and I needed to head home. I had to get up early to go help out at Kris's shop. Giving the girls the "look", they caught my drift and we got ready to go. Maine stood up from the couch at the same time as me. I thought nothing as I went to walk towards the door until he pulled me back by my arm. I looked him up and down, confused as to why he was manhandling me.

"Can I get your number?" He said it in a whisper like he didn't want everyone else to hear. My initial response was to tell him to speak up, but I didn't wanna be an asshole.

"Sure, gimme ya phone." He handed it to me, and I typed in my number before calling myself. "There you go. Have a good night and be safe." By now Mecca and Shanice were walking out the door and I followed.

"Shawty swing my wayyy, sho look good to me, now would you please swing my wayyy, shawty swing my wayyy," Mecca sang as she did an updated tootsie roll. Shanice laughed and I shook my head. "This was a good idea, Sha. Gave cutie my number and Kaia slid Maine her number on the low." I couldn't hide shit from her ass.

After dropping them both off, I headed home to get some sleep. Taking off my clothes, I took a quick shower and put a scarf on my head to hold my ponytail as I slept. Picking up my phone, I texted the girls to let them know I got home safe just as a text from an unsaved number came through.

917-371-2725: *You made it home okay?*

Me: *Who's this?*

917-371-2725: *Damn, you ain't lock me in yet? It's Maine.*

Me: *Oh, my bad, let me do it now.*

I saved his number under *Rude Ass* and went back to texting. We texted back and forth, getting to know each other before I eventually fell asleep...with him on my mind.

MY ALARM WENT off at nine a.m., scaring me half to death. I knew I couldn't just hit the snooze button and go back to bed. Kris would surely curse my ass out and I didn't feel like going through that with her. Jumping up, I made my bed and freshened up. Throwing on a pair of cut up jean shorts, a Lacoste Polo, and a pair of all white Uptowns, I grabbed one of my many cross-body bags and left my room.

"Morning y'all," I greeted both my parents in a lively tone.

"Hey love, you on your way to the shop?" My mother inquired, standing at the stove, making breakfast.

"Yeah, just for a few hours, though."

"Okay, be safe." Kissing both of their cheeks, I headed out the door. I made it to the shop at the same time as Kris and Heaven were pulling up.

"Alright now, you better be on time ya first day on the job," Heaven said, hugging me.

"Uhn, uhn, I do not work here. I'm just helping out. Sis, what's wrong with you?" I asked Kris whose face held a frown.

"Oh, she is not having a good morning. She had to change her number *again* because not only is Kane playing on her phone, but he done tagged China's ass in, too." My sister couldn't catch a damn break when it came to Kane's ass.

"I don't wanna talk about it. Come on, let's get in here and open up." I dropped the subject and got ready to work.

For most of the day, I helped shampoo, answered phones, and swept. Most of the stuff that Kris's receptionist would do, but she was on vacation. Either way, I didn't mind helping. I'd been clocked in for a few hours before I got a text from Maine, requesting I come outside. Setting the broom that I used to sweep down, I went outside to find him sitting on the hood of a BMW i8.

He looked so good in his plain white-T, Balmain jeans, and all white Uptowns that looked like today was their first debut out the box; similar to mine. It was something bout a dude in a fresh white-T that got my attention. Making my way over, I stopped in front of him, and stood between his legs. We stared at each other for a few seconds, his face straight, while I tried to figure out what was going through his head at this moment. I didn't know why I was so attracted to his rude ass, but I was.

"What you doing here?"

"I don't know, shorty. I was driving and somehow ended up here."

"Oh yeah? I'm not gon' keep telling you about that shorty shit," I checked him with a smile. I'd concluded that he was gon' keep calling me *shorty* regardless of how I felt.

"Come take a ride with me." He urged completely disregarding what I said.

"I can't, my sister needs me today," I declined.

"Yes, you can. I already spoke to ya sister. You good for the rest of the day. Go grab ya bag, I'ma be in the car." He hopped down from the hood, kissed my forehead, and went to sit in the driver's seat.

We'd reached the *kissing on the forehead* stage rather quickly. I wasn't gonna be the one to complain. Heading back to the shop to ask Kris if I could leave for a few hours, before I could push the door open, she was walking over with my purse in her hand.

"Here you go, sis. Have fun and call me when you get to your destination and when you get home." The smile on her face said that she set me up, but I wasn't mad. I actually wanted to go out with Maine. Something about the text conversation last night allowed me to let my guard down a little bit.

"Make him pay for everything. Anything happen to my cousin, that's yo' ass, Maine!" Heaven shouted from inside the shop. We both laughed as hopped in on the passenger side and he sped off.

"So, where we going?" I asked as he weaved through the mid-day traffic.

"I ain't gon' lie, I didn't have a destination in mind. I just wanted you to ride with me."

I laughed at his honesty. "You know you bogus as hell for that, right? Let's go to The Boil downtown. Oh wait, we didn't make a reservation, never mind."

"No reservation needed when you're with a boss, shorty," he said cockily.

"No plans either, apparently," I shot back, smirking. He

grinned and shrugged his shoulders. The Boil didn't have too much of a crowd when we arrived, so we were able to get a seat by the window. He pulled out my chair and once I was seated comfortably, he took a seat of his own.

"You got a girl, Maine?"

He looked caught off guard by the question but recovered quickly. "Nah, you?"

"Nah, I don't swing that way." I kept a straight face for as long as I could before giggling.

"You know what I mean." He laughed with me.

"Oh, a man? Nope, I don't."

"Good, I didn't wanna have to break up no happy home."

"What makes you think I'd let you, if I was in a relationship?" I countered.

"You wouldn't have *let* me do nothing. I would've approached yo' dude on some man-to-man shit. It wouldn't have taken nothing to get him on the same page." I wanted to give a slick response but was interrupted.

"Damn, that's how you gon' do my girl, Maine?" Unique, one of Kandice's pits, spoke to Maine.

"Who yo' girl?" He shot back, confused.

I watched both of them to see how the conversation would play out. This was the prime example for why I wasn't sweating being in a relationship. The waitress walked over while Unique stared a hole in the side of Maine's face. I acted as if she wasn't there and ordered my food. Shit, I wasn't gonna miss out on a good meal for nobody.

"Don't play dumb in front of this bitch." She pointed in my direction and I took it as her calling me out. I planned to stay out of it, but she invited me in and who was I to decline the invitation?

"This the bitch that's gon' go across yo' shit if you don't move yo' finger from my direction," I promised. My hands didn't discriminate at all. Man, woman, or animal in her case, could get this work. She knew she didn't want these problems, so she continued with Maine.

"I'ma go. You betta believe I'll be letting Kandice know about this shit, though." She walked away, leaving me stuck. Are you fucking kidding me? *Kandice* of all people. Now I knew why I needed to steer clear of him.

Ant

Ever since I spent the night with Kristen, we had been inseparable. At this point, she was my girl if anyone asked. She knew it and I knew it; we just hadn't made a verbal confirmation as of yet. Today was a step towards it. It was signing day for Promise Records and she'd taken the day off to be by my side.

"I'm so proud of you, babe," she expressed, excitedly, hugging me around my neck.

"Thank you, ma. I appreciate you being here today." I kissed her neck and she giggled.

"We should go out tonight and celebrate. Not no regular

dinner either. Let's go out to a lounge or something and have a drink."

"I'm wit it. Call up ya girls, I'ma call my niggas, and it's a gangsta celebration." I was one step closer to being done with the streets, a turn up was well deserved.

After solidifying everything with my lawyer, I dropped Kris off at home so I could run a few errands before we met up again later. Before leaving her, I made sure to let her know that Kaia needed to be in attendance. I didn't want to hear Maine talking his bullshit if his shorty wasn't there. She agreed that she would make it happen. We kissed and I watched as she entered her building.

Once she confirmed that she had made it in her apartment, I pulled off. Although we hadn't done the naked two step, I still wanted to be under shorty whenever I had free time. I actually liked that she was making me wait. It let me know that pussy and a cute face weren't all she had to offer. Chilling with her was like being with one of the guys. She talked big shit, played sports, and could cook. My baby was the shit. Picking up my phone, I called up Maine to let him know that we were celebrating tonight.

"**What?!**" He barked into the phone.

"**Nigga, fix yo' tone when you see me calling. Fuck is yo' problem?**" I swear this nigga was bipolar. I had just spoken to him earlier and he seemed fine.

"**Nothing, man, wassup, what you need? And nigga, this my fuckin' phone, I'll answer this shit how I want to.**"

"**I need you to fix yo' attitude and stop acting like a female. I signed the papers to the building a few minutes ago, so we going out to celebrate. I don't wanna hear shit, you going.**" I wasn't taking no for an answer. He was the first artist on the label and my partner. This celebration was just as much his as it was mine.

"**Yeah, whateva man. I need to get Rel and Kelsey situated first.**" Bro had stepped up in a major way for Lil' Rel and his sister. My mother had taken a liking to them immediately, especially Kelsey. They were with her more than at the apartment.

"**Aight, I'll hit you later and tell you the meet up time.**"

"**Yo', is Kaia gonna be there?**" He asked, sounding hopeful. The last time I checked they were getting along, so I was confused by the question.

"**I told Kristen to make sure of it. But, call her, that's *yo' shorty.***" He got quiet and I pressed the issue to find out what all he wasn't telling me. "**What happened?**"

"**What you mean?**"

"**I mean, you asking if Kaia gon' be in attendance like you blocked from her phone or something. So, what happened?**"

He sucked his teeth. "**Nothing. Hit me when you en route to the location.**"

"**Aight, man.**" He was the first to hang up.

I couldn't be concerned with Maine's lovesick, confused ass. With a few hours to kill before getting the night started, I made my way to Kutz barbershop to get a line up. My mans Ace and his cousin owned the place. I fucked with them; they were some thorough niggas. Pulling up, there was a dice game going on in front of the shop. It was about seven dudes and one woman who had the dice in her hand. The woman was talking cash shit. I moved closer so I could see what was in the pot. I wanted in on the action.

"Aight, young niggas, lemme show you how they gave me the nickname *headcrack* back in the 70's." My mom's voice was clear as day. All I could do was shake my head at this lady with money in one hand and shaking the dice in the other.

"Ma, you serious right now?" The crowd looked my way and Ace was amongst the group, unbelievable.

"Not right now, baby, I'ma 'bout to buy me a new pair of shoes on one of these fellas here." She blew on the dice before throwing them to the ground, hitting a seven. "Run me my money, PERIODT." The guys grumbled under their breath but made sure to hand over the cash.

"Ain't this some shit. Ma Jane, you out here with them fake dice?" Ace complained while the guys laughed.

"Nigga, these yo' dice," she retorted.

"Oh, you right." We all laughed at Ace and he shook his head, joining in. Walking over to give me a pound, he kissed my mom's cheek.

"I keep tellin' you lil' niggas stop putting y'all lips on my face. I know y'all be out here up to no good with these females."

"Nah, Ma Jane," Ace went to defend himself. "I'm only up to no good with one female. Like, I do her bad bad."

"Boy, get the hell on," she swatted him.

"What you doing up here?" I asked.

"Had to bring Jhareel to get a cut. He should be almost done now." I held the door open for her and we walked in.

"Y'all finished getting y'all ass handed to y'all by the OG?" My barber, Big Boy, clowned. Ace responded with the finger while my mom snickered. I gave Rel a pound, who was sitting in the seat getting a cut, and let Big Boy know I needed a quick line. While waiting, I received a text from Detective Kane, letting me know that it was urgent that he spoke with me. He knew we didn't do the back-and-forth texting, so I didn't respond. This man was steady acting like we were cool and shit.

"You know ya brother been walking around sulking for the past few days about that Kaia girl," my mom mentioned, taking a seat next to me.

"Oh yeah?" I thought back to the phone call and the sour mood he seemed to be in.

"Yep. I think she done broke my baby's heart. You need to fix this before I have to whip her little ass." I had to laugh at her threat.

"How you gon' threaten the girl and you don't even know what happened?"

"Cause that's my baby and he seemed so jovial before. Fix this for mama and I wanna meet these two girls that got y'all so smitten, especially you." I smiled big, thinking about Kris. I would definitely be setting up that meeting sooner than later. An hour later, my line up was fresh, and I headed to the mall to cop me an outfit for tonight.

I WAS able to pull some strings at Amadeus in Queens to get Kaia in the club, being that she wasn't 21. Clearly, she didn't have much of a beef with bro like he thought, seeing that she came out tonight. Kris was looking good as hell in a black dress that had her whole back on display when she turned around. The shit looked like a second layer of skin, the way it fit her body. For the first time, I noticed a single red rose tattoo she had in the middle of her back. It looked so delicate, I wanted to place a trail of soft kisses along the outline of it. The plan was to make sure she wasn't too far for me to reach out and touch her. She was sure to get a nigga bodied with what she had on.

The section we had was big enough for fifty people even though we had about thirty. The DJ spinned all the latest records and I sat back watching Kris dance and the niggas watch. I wanted to have a good night, so as long as they admired from afar I was good. Bro had finally pulled up at a quarter to twelve. Now it was time to get the party cracking.

"Everybody grab a glass so we can toast this shit up." I waited for everyone to take a glass from the tray and pulled Kris close to me. "This toast is to *Promise Records*. We about to take this shit to a whole other level. Bro, with you, we already got the game on smash. Thank you for trusting me with your skills. We taking this shit all the way." He put his hand over his chest, signaling respect. We clinked glasses and everybody went wild with congratulations and applause.

Before we could set our glasses back down gun shots rang throughout the club. ***Ratatatatatatatat.*** I instinctively pushed Kris down to the ground and Maine followed suit with Kaia. I didn't need to instruct the crew on what to do. I had a bunch of hittas on my team, so they bust back with no hesitation, exchanging round after round.

"Stay down, you hear me?" I instructed Kris and Kaia who nodded in understanding.

Both their eyes were wide, and I could tell they were scared. They held it down, though. Standing up, I pulled out my hammer and engaged in the gun fire, doing my best not to hit any innocent people. I took notice of three hooded individuals who had stopped shooting at us, once they realized they were outnumbered. The club was in an uproar. Snatching Kris up by her arm, I pulled her to the exit.

"My sister!" She shouted, trying to pull away from me, but was unsuccessful due to the tight grip I had on her arm.

"Maine got her, ma. I promise."

"I don't think you understand. I'm not going NOWHERE

WITHOUT MY SISTER!" She held her ground just like I would've about my brother.

"Aight, at least let me get you to the car and we'll call her. Come on, ma, trust me. Them niggas might be lurking, and I can't lose you." She gave me that at least and we made it to my car where she called Kaia. Kaia answered on the first ring, confirming that she was good and with Maine like I said. We sped off with her holding my hand tightly. Just when I thought I was in the clear to step off from this street shit, these niggas drag me back in.

Kristen

We were having such a good time at the club and then the shots rang out. I could still feel my ears ringing. Antwon was a fool to think I was leaving that club without Kaia Monique Phillips. After ensuring she was good, my heart started to settle a little. In the car, we drove in silence. I held onto his hand tightly and squeezed it every few seconds. It felt like he was gonna disappear at any moment and my heart tightened at the thought.

"I'm right here, ma. I ain't going nowhere," he declared, seemingly able to read my mind. He kissed my hand and kept driving.

I knew we weren't going to my house as we ventured into Westchester. It didn't matter where we went. Right now, in this moment, I wanted to be up under him. I took a minute to text Kaia to make sure she was good with Maine. She replied that she was good, and he was getting on her nerves acting like she was shot, and complaining about her choice of outfit. I laughed out loud; I thought her jean jumpsuit was cute. It made her booty look hella big.

"What you over there laughing about?"

"Yo' brother harassing my sister about what she had on tonight. He's a trip."

"Well shit, you got yo' whole back out and I know niggas were out there drooling over you. I caught myself doing the same," he admitted, making me smile.

"I wore this little number for you. I wanted to make a statement."

"You made it, ma. That's for damn sure." He missed the subtle sexual hint in my statement.

We arrived at a nice brick house that I assumed was his. Since we'd been hanging out, we mainly chilled at my place or went out somewhere. He got out and came around front to open my door. Placing my hand in his, I stepped out and closed the door behind me. I loved the cobble stone ground leading up to the door. I prayed that my stilettos wouldn't give out on me as I walked. The Jimmy Choo heels I'd worn had done their job and gotten me this far, and I didn't need them failing me now.

Stepping through the door, he hung his keys on the wall and bent down in front of me. I moved back a little, not knowing what he was doing. When he reached for my shoe, I was impressed. He removed them both and grabbed my hand to walk me further into the house. It was beautiful, very spacious for just him and his daughter. While I wanted to take a tour, he grabbed my hand and led me upstairs.

"You need anything?" He asked when we made it to where I assumed was his bedroom. I shook my head. "You wanna take a shower?" I shook my head again. "Use ya words, ma."

"I want you to fuck me." I shocked myself with the words that came out of my mouth, but I'd been thinking about it for a while.

He responded by placing his lips on mine. As he kissed me, his fingers danced up and down my exposed back, causing a tingling sensation to go throughout my body. I loved to kiss, and I especially loved kissing him. Leaning my head back, I let him suck on my neck and bite me, sure to leave a mark. The puddle in my thong let me know just how much I didn't care. "Mmmm." I bit my lip while reaching for his shirt to pull it off.

He detached his lips from my neck and assisted me. "Alexa, play *Forever I'm Ready* by Jeremiah," he called out to the surround sound system. I slipped out of my dress and thong with little to no effort and took his hand in mine, placing it on my pussy so he could see how wet I was.

I guess I'm for you, baby, I want to know you, lady. Told you I'm different, don't you act distant, forever I'm readyyy.

Dancing to the beat, I grinded on his hand and he licked his lips. The friction between my dancing and his hand moving back and forth on my clit made me throw my head back in ecstasy. Kissing me again, he backed me up against the wall and bent down in front of me, never moving his hand from my pussy. Lifting my leg, it rested on his shoulder. Before I could prepare myself, his tongue was on me, sucking on my clit ever so softly.

"Ooh, yesss, Antwon," I whimpered as he slurped at my pussy like it was his favorite fruit. He was so gentle and methodical with it. I swore I felt my eyes roll in the back of my head. I couldn't help but grind into his mouth when he started to lick from my pussy to my asshole. Swirling his tongue around my ass, he made slurping noises, making me even wetter. "Arghhh... wait," my legs shook, and he held onto me, his tongue grabbing hold of my clit again.

"Mmmm, damn girl, what you eating? This pussy good as hell," he complimented while turning me around to where I had my hands on the wall.

I went to respond but he latched back onto me, this time with my ass on his face. I felt his fingers start playing in my wetness and I lost it. I braced myself as I came so hard, it leaked down my legs. He lapped up every bit of it before standing up and carrying me over to the bed. Sitting down on the edge of his California king, I unbuckled his pants and released his dick.

The same color as him, it stood at attention like it knew what was gonna happen next. The veins that pulsated in his dick had my mouth watering. He was so thick, that I couldn't wrap my whole hand around him, but I was up for the challenge of wrapping my mouth around it. I looked in his eyes as I licked along his shaft. Spitting on it, I stroked him with my hands before licking around the head.

"Mmhmm," he moaned and nodded. Deciding it was enough of getting to know my new friend, I took him in my mouth as much as I could and sucked him up real good. My gag reflexes were apparent, but I took it like a champ. Feeling my eyes water, I knew he'd tapped the back of my throat. "Oohh fuck," he groaned, grabbing my head and sliding in and out of my mouth slowly so not to choke me. I felt spit coming out the side of my mouth and kept my eyes on his that were now closed. When they popped open, I didn't know if it was the look that I was giving him that turned him on or if the head was just that good, but he pulled out and shot his load on my titties. "Shitttt, my bad, ma. That tongue is lethal."

I was a freak, so I didn't mind. Right now, I wanted the dick. We could worry about cleaning me up later. Taking charge, I grabbed his dick and guided him into my sticky pussy. My body tensed a little with his size, but I got used to it fast. He made sure not to put all his weight on me as he intensely stroked my middle, making me wetter with each thrust.

"Yeahhh, keep that pussy juicy for me, ma. I'ma make her cum real good, baby." His sex talk turned me on even more. I opened my legs further so I could get all of him and he smirked. "Oh, you want me to fuck this pussy, huh?" He gave my pussy a light slap and a deep moan escaped me.

I knew my face displayed my complete and utter desire for him to fuck me until I couldn't take anymore. He responded by pushing my legs out as far as they could go, raising up on his knees, and going balls deep in me. We went at it for an hour, cumming back-to-back, and ended the night on the floor, with me laying in the crook of his arm.

"You know we official, right?" I heard him say as my eyelids got heavy.

"I know," I confirmed and snuggled closer to him before dosing off.

It was nine in the morning when I woke up to my phone going off. We were no longer on the floor but resting comfortably in his bed. Antwon was dead to the world, with one leg on me and his hand comfortably rested on my titty. I snickered because it was a sight to see. Careful not to wake him, I moved his hand from my titty but was unsuccessful in getting his heavy ass leg off me. Doing the best I could, I reached over and grabbed it from his nightstand.

"Kris, get yo' ass up!" Heaven yelled in my ear.

"I'm up, I'm up." I tried my best not to sound sleepy.

"The hell you are. You know we supposed to call each other when we get home from an outing. Even Kaia had the decency to call."

"I'm sorry, boo. Last night was too crazy." I squeezed my legs closed just thinking about the hurting Antwon had put on my pussy.

"I know, Kaia told me about the shooting. Are you okay?" She was understandably concerned.

"Oh, that, yeah, I'm good."

"Hmph okay, so where you at right now?"

"At daddy's house, 'bout to get that ass tapped again!" Antwon blurted out, clearly ear hustling. I pushed him back and scurried out of the bed before he could make good on what he had just said.

"Girl, ignore his ass."

Heaven got a kick of it as she released a fit of giggles. "Well tear it up then. I'ma talk to you later, girl." She hung up quickly.

Antwon had a sneaky smile on his face, getting out of bed and heading into the bathroom. He didn't know if I wanted Heaven all in my business. I mean, of course I was gonna tell her, but damn. Setting my phone back down, I decided to take a quick shower before heading home. I always carried an extra pair of panties in my bag, not because I was on no hoe shit either. It was for emergencies. I wasn't the girl that could free ball and I wasn't putting on the same underwear I had juiced up in, that's for damn sure.

I was now very comfortable with Ant, especially after he had explored my insides last night, so I walked into the bathroom in my birthday suit. Seeing that the shower was on, I figured he was prepared to do the same. He looked at me through the massive mirror that was over the his and her bathroom sinks. My hair was all over my head and I did my best to finger-comb through. Reaching over, he moved my hands from my head.

"You still the shit, ma." I smiled as he licked my top lip before tap-kissing me. It was all I could offer since my breath was on tart time. "You wanna get in the shower with me?"

Covering my mouth, I answered, "Yeah, let me just brush my teeth real quick." He snickered and pointed to the toothbrush on the sink.

After handling my mouth, I got into the shower with him. We joked around and washed each other from head to toe. Before we got out, he ate my pussy for breakfast. Had a bitch feeling like she could conquer the world. I got dressed in my underwear and t-shirt and we lounged around the house being that I didn't have to go into the shop.

While watching reruns of *My Wife and Kids,* my phone rang. Checking the caller ID, I saw an *unknown* caller displayed. Sighing loudly, I hit ignore. I knew it was Kane without having to answer. Changing my number had become a joke. Antwon looked at me and I mustered up a phony smile. Before I could cuddle back up to him, a text message came through.

929-682-4567: *Answer your phone, Kristen.*

Another call came through and I ignored that one, too. Then there was another text.

929-682-4567: *Alright, I see how you wanna play. You laid up with that nigga, Ant. I got something for yo' ass.*

What the fuck? How did he know who I was with? So much for newfound happiness.

Maine

Kaia still wasn't fucking with me even after I had practically saved her life. The gun shots from tonight were directed right at our section. My instincts kicked in immediately as I dived on top of her. She didn't cry or yell like a scared woman usually would. That's when I knew she was in a state of shock. She said nothing the entire time I led her out the club and into my car. In fact, she only spoke when Kris called to check on her. Once she noticed we weren't headed to her crib, she spoke up.

"Umm, I don't live this way." I kept driving, now giving her ass the silent treatment to see how she liked it. "Maine, I know you hear me talking to you."

"Yep, and I know you hear me ignoring you like you did me." I knew I was being childish, but fuck it. I heard her chuckle and looked her way. This girl was crazy as hell, a good crazy, though. "You really laughing? You trippin', shorty."

"I'm only laughing because you pouting like a baby. For real, though. Where we going?"

"I have to stop by my mom's then I'm taking you to my house."

She didn't put up a fuss like I thought she would, so I kept in the direction I was going. I needed to check in on Rel and Kelsey. I made sure to tap in with them every day, sometimes a few times throughout the day. Usually, I would call, but with it being this late, and after what had gone down at the club, I needed to see their faces. They had only been with me a couple days, but I was attached to them before then.

"Wait," she grabbed at my arm. "We really going to ya mama's house at this time? It's late as hell." I looked at her with a look that said, *and*? She sucked her teeth and shook her head. I could hear her mumbling under her breath, calling me all kinds of dumb asses. I laughed silently and pulled into my mother's driveway. She was sure to cuss me out. First, Ant came to the house all late with Bre, now I was coming in late with a woman.

I put my car in park and got out. Kaia sat in the car with her arms crossed. Now, who was the one pouting? I bent down and knocked on the passenger side window. She glanced in my direction and turned her head straight again. Pulling on the door handle, I opened the door and held out my hand for her to grab. Stubbornly, she did.

"This outfit too damn tight, shorty." She frowned and sucked her teeth.

"You don't worry 'bout what I got on. Worry about Kandice and her fashions. Move. Come on and let's get this over with it." The sensors that came up in the driveway must've woken my mother because she was at the door with her robe on and her .380 by her side.

"You and ya brother are some disrespectful ass people. Sometimes I wonder who raised y'all niggas. Why y'all keep thinking it's okay to pop up at my damn house any time of night?" Before I could say anything in response, she held up her hand. "Pretty girl, what are you doing out this time of night?" She directed her attention to Kaia who had clammed up and tried to hide behind me.

"Ma, this..."

"She got a mouth, don't she?" I nodded and closed mine. "Well, then, she can answer. Come on around here, pretty, and speak when spoken to." I pulled Kaia by her hand and placed her in front of me.

"Umm, hi Ms. Brown, my name is Kaia."

"You can call me Ma Jane just like everybody else. Oh my, this is yo' Kaia, huh, son?" Leave it to her to call me out like I talked about shorty all the time. Kaia looked to me with furrowed brows. "You did good, son. Come on in here, Kaia.

You look too young to be out this late, but I'ma let you slide because I know there's a good reason for it. Ain't that right, Tremaine?"

"Really? The government name though, Ma?"

"Boy, bring yo' ass in this house," she scolded, and Kaia laughed, following behind her as I brought up the rear.

"That shit ain't funny and don't you dare think you 'bout to be calling me that," I whispered from behind her.

She looked back at me with a smirk. "Alright, Tremaine. You got it."

They went to the kitchen while I went to find Kelsey and Rel. Checking in on Kelsey first, she was sleeping peacefully in Bre's room, while Rel was across the hall in the guest bedroom knocked out.

"You know, sooner or later, these kids have to go back to they mama, right? No matter how much I enjoy them being here, they have a mama."

I heard my mother's voice from behind me but didn't bother turning around. I knew I couldn't keep them. I didn't think I was stable or worthy enough to be their sole provider. Something in me did wonder what life would be like if I had them full time, though. "You and Kaia spend the night. I don't want y'all out driving this late. Oh, and you can tell me in the morning what happened that made you come by here at almost two in the morning." She walked off and I gave Rel one last glance before following her.

I overheard Kaia laughing softly in the kitchen with my

mom and stood at the entryway watching them interact. Kaia looked comfortable with her and that was everything in my book. I wanted my mama to love my girl. I mean, she wasn't my girl yet, but... she was...shit, I didn't know. I stayed back and listened as my mother talked about me growing up.

"Babyyy, Tremaine was a pissy ass little boy. He would wet the bed and then attempt to change the sheets himself so I wouldn't notice. I'd catch him every time because he would forget to change his underwear, too." Both her and Kaia got in good laughs at my expense. "Ain't that right, baby boy?" She caught me ear hustling.

"Nah, I don't recall, Mama." I plead the fifth. Kaia couldn't stop laughing as I nudged her. The shit wasn't that funny.

"Uh huh, well, I'ma get to bed. I already told Tremaine y'all was spending the night and don't try to argue with me, lil' Miss Kaia." I could tell she was ready to protest, but moms wasn't having it. "Goodnight, see y'all in the morning." She kissed my forehead and did the same with Kaia. Ahhh, she was *officially* in there. I smiled goofily and Kaia smirked.

"That don't mean nothing." I guess she caught onto what I was thinking. "And where will I be resting my pretty head?" I nodded toward the back and walked off. Opening the door to my bedroom, she looked at me and frowned. "Oh, so you got the floor. Copy, that's cool with me." She had me fucked up if she thought I was sleeping on the floor in my own room.

"Nah, shorty, we sleeping in this King sized joint together. Here's a t-shirt and a fresh pair of boxers. Go make it do what it do."

I pointed towards the bathroom and she pouted before stomping off. I don't know what she was acting all pissy for, she knew she wanted to sleep up under a nigga. While I waited for her to finish in the shower, I checked my messages. There was one from bro making sure I was good and what looked like an essay from Kandice. Hitting bro back first, I let him know everything was everything and I was at Mamas.

Kandice had me fucked up if she thought I was reading that long ass message. iPhone had the voice note feature for a reason. I closed out of her text thread and went on IG to see if there was anything interesting happening there. Again, the same ol' shit, so I logged out. Hearing Kaia clearing her throat, I looked up.

"Where can I put my underwear?" She asked with a pair of lace panties dangling from her hand. Oh, shorty was hood, she straight washed her shits out by hand. I laughed at her zero fucks attitude. "What happened, why you laughing?"

"Nothing, shorty. That was just some real shit you did. You can hang them over the shower, in the bathroom." She did like I suggested and came back to sit on the bed.

Handing her the remote, I went to shower myself. She scooted up on the bed, making my t-shirt lift up, exposing her meaty thighs. Her skin looked so damn soft. I must've been staring too long because she quickly pulled the cover over her. Chuckling, I went to handle my business.

I took a long shower, too. A nigga was all over the place after seeing just a little thigh. These Phillips girls must have some kind of damn spell on them. Antwon was far gone, and I felt myself falling, too. My usual fifteen-minute shower turned into twenty-five. Once I was out, I felt like my mind was back in the right place. I came out with my towel wrapped around my waist and she was laying on her side on her phone.

"You good?"

"Yep," she answered, short.

"You sure?" I pried further, unsure why. She popped up quickly.

"Nah, I ain't good. Why Kandice calling yo' phone this late?" Her arms were folded across her chest and her hair that was once out, framing her face, was now pulled back in a ponytail. I found it cute that she was jealous, so I decided to fuck with her.

"Why you checking my phone like you my girl?" I smiled, waiting for her answer.

"Boy please, I know I ain't yo' girl. It was ringing and woke me up out my sleep." I cracked up laughing at her lying ass. My phone had been on vibrate since the club.

"Oh yeah?"

"Yeah," she countered with confidence like she wasn't flat out lying.

"Well, my bad." I let my towel drop, giving her an eye full of this grown man dick. She sucked her teeth and turned away. Again, I snickered and slipped on a pair of boxers before getting in the bed with my back to her. "Goodnight, Kaia."

"You rude as hell. That's why I don't like yo' ass." She mushed the back of my head and turned around, pulling the covers with her. I smiled because she'd reacted just like I wanted her to. Pulling at her arm, I turned her body to face me.

"You wanna be my girl, shorty?"

"What? No. Hell no!" She looked everywhere but at me when she responded. I grabbed her face and covered her lips with mine. Pulling her bottom lip in between my teeth, I rubbed on her booty underneath the cover. The feeling was different. I had only kissed one girl in my life, and it was a crush I had in elementary. After that, I was just fucking so there was no point in kissing.

"You wanna be my girl, Kaia?" I asked again and this time she nodded. "What that mean?"

"Yes, Tremaine, I wanna be ya girl." I let her get a pass on calling me by my government when she gave me that pretty ass smile.

"Don't get too comfortable calling me that name. My mama was out of line." I kissed her again, loving the feeling of her lips on mine.

"I'm ya girl?"

"Hell yeah."

"Then I'ma call you Tremaine when I want to." She put her hand up to my face and rubbed my cheek.

Pulling her hand back, I kissed her open palm. "Oh, I can't wait to show you just how much you don't run shit round here. Come on and let's go to sleep for I stick something in you." She glanced down at my hard on, gave a lazy smirk, and turned around.

I cuddled her from behind and fell into a deep, peaceful slumber.

Kaia

When I went to sleep, I was in Maine's arms and when I woke up this morning, I was in bed alone. Not only had I slept in bed with him at his mama's house, but I agreed to be his girl. I can tell you I didn't expect the night to end the way that it did. I couldn't say that I wasn't happy about it, though. We had made it official, but we still needed to have the Kandice conversation. I'd leave it alone for the moment.

Quickly redressing in what I had on the night before, including my panties that I hand washed, I checked my phone for any missed messages. Seeing one from my mom, I let her know I'd be home soon. I also texted Kris to see where she was. She let me know she was still with Antwon and would be by the house to see me later. Up and ready, I didn't want to walk through Maine's mama's house, so I texted him to come to the room. He did a few seconds later.

"Wassup, scary," he joked, taking a seat on the bed next to me.

"Shut up. I need a toothbrush and I need to get home soon."

"I left one in the bathroom for you. Come down when you done so you can get some food in ya stomach, then I can drop you off." He went to stand, but I grabbed his hand.

"Wait for me. I don't wanna go down by myself. Ya mama gon' think we was in here hunching and I'm doing the walk of shame." I was not for looking like some hoe. He laughed like I said something funny.

"Shorty, you good. She knows you ain't let me sniff it yet. Plus, my mama would kick my ass if I had you screaming and moaning up in her house." His cocky, nasty ass just had to be extra.

"Boy whateva, just wait for me." I went to handle my mouth and rinse my face. When I returned to the room he was in the same spot, but on his phone. I wanted to say something smart but decided I didn't want to be perceived as the jealous girl. I had already made that mistake last night.

"All good?"

"Yep."

"Oh, wait...let me get you right." He reached into the draw on the nightstand and pulled out a jar of Vaseline. "Here you go."

"It get lonely some nights, huh?" I laughed and he mushed my head.

"Girl, mind yo business and grease yo face. Actually, let me do it." He scooped a little of the Vaseline into his palm and gently rubbed it in my face. The gesture wasn't sensual but...loving...different. Once he was satisfied, he kissed my lips twice and grabbed my hand. "Come on."

We entered the dining room together where there was a big spread set up. Seated at the table with his mom were the two kids I saw with him at BBQs.

"Hey, it's the pretty girl we saw at the restaurant, Rely," the little girl pointed at her brother who confirmed.

"Yeah, her name is Kaia, Kels. Hey, how you doing?" He spoke to me.

"I'm good, Rel. And you are very beautiful as well, Kelsey." I smiled at her cute, oval face. She pat the seat next to her for me to sit, while Maine sat across from me, next to Rel.

"I'm glad to see everyone here," Ma Jane spoke as she came in with a pitcher of orange juice. "I hope you slept well, Kaia."

"I did. Thank you for letting me stay."

"No problem, love. Now that you and Maine are all boo'd up, you're welcome here anytime."

I looked to Maine who smiled and shrugged his shoulders. He thought he was so slick. I thought it was cute that he told his mom about us, though. After we ate, I said my goodbyes and promised Kelsey a trip to the Trolls Experience soon. That little girl was everything. I didn't quite understand why they were in Maine's care, so I asked during the ride to my house.

"Are you close with Rel and Kelsey's mom?"

"Nah, she's a crackhead that's not responsible. Rel has been basically taking care of his little sister until I came along. I look out for them and shit. I just paid for their mom to do a ninety-day program at a rehab center my cousin owns. That'll give her time to get her shit together before they go back to school." I looked at him in awe once he finished talking. Here he was, twenty-years-old, taking in kids when he had his own life to live.

"That's dope. Any way I can help, I'm here." We were parked at a red light, so I took the opportunity to lean over and kiss his soft lips. I sat back, blushing as he pulled off. We had a little ride to my house, so I sat back and listened to Dani Leigh's *Easy* remix featuring Chris Brown.

Damn, we so fire babe, whippin' through the 305 highway, love it how you ride in the fast lane, make me wanna say, that's my bae. Dani gotta behave, gotta be chill like a Sunday. Never wanna look too thirsty, but your drip got me feeling wavy.

Dani had explained just how I felt about Maine in a nutshell. Music had a way of conveying your feelings without you having to do any talking. The song was cut off by his phone that rang through his Bluetooth. It was Kandice calling. I sighed, looking over at him. I was almost positive that he was gonna dub her call, being that he was with me, but to my surprise, he answered.

"Yo'," he said with annoyance.

"Oh, so it's *fuck me* now?" She spat.

I whispered, *duh* to the air as if she was standing in front of me.

"Kandice, we ain't rocking like that so wassup, man?"

"Oh, now we ain't rocking like that? Since when? Let me guess, since you been fucking with Kaia's wack ass, huh?"

My lip twitched. I wanted to say something so bad, but I wanted to see how he was going to handle the situation. With me being his girl now, it was critical that he handled her accordingly.

"For one, watch how you speak on *my* woman. Two, I'm off the market... *officially*. So, when you or ya homegirls see me in the streets, keep that in mind." I smiled big and grabbed his hand.

"Yeah aight, nigga, we'll see. Kaia ain't giving up the pussy, with her virgin ass. I'll see you when you ready to get ya dick wet." She hung up the phone abruptly. I absentmindedly let his hand go because that was the one thing that she had to offer that I didn't, *pussy*.

"Don't let that shit get to you, shorty. If all a woman has to offer is pussy, then she ain't got nothing to offer." He put my hand in his again and held it until we pulled up in front of my building. I went to get out but he stopped me. "You gon' get out and not let me feel ya lips again? You cold, girlfriend."

I snickered, getting back in the car. I touched his cheek and pecked his lips, which wasn't enough for him because he grabbed the back of my head and deepened the kiss. "Mmmm," I moaned into his mouth, feeling myself getting moist. I pulled back first to get myself together. "I'll call you later, boyfriend."

"Aight, text me when you get in, though." I nodded and got out the car. Kandice was gon' have to pack it up. I was craving me some Maine and I couldn't shake the feeling.

MY RELATIONSHIP PROGRESSED RATHER QUICKLY and Maine and I were now three months in. He was everything I didn't expect him to be. He was taking the time to get to know my flaws, my dreams, and my pet peeves. Things that I thought he would have no interest in, he was open to experiencing because it made me happy. I could honestly say I had learned a lot about him as well. We were spending a lot of time together and my girls encouraged it, seeing as they were going just as hard in their newfound relationships.

I had even gone as far as gifting him my virginity a couple weeks back. And baby, when you put yo' stuff in the right hands and they do it right, you'd love him a long time. He made me feel so special that night in more ways than one. I was a quick learner and by round three, I had shown him a few tricks of my own. Those sporadic visits to different porn sites had been educational for me.

Today, Ant was throwing a talent show at the Kingdome to scout new talent for Promise Records. I was geeked because my baby was going to be performing his single "The One" at the show. He had been going hard promoting his mix tape and it was paying off. My man was on the radio and everything.

"Y'all need to come on," I fussed at Mecca and Shanice as I checked myself out in the full-length mirror. They had spent the night at my house the night before so that we could head out to the park together. I wanted to be a little flashy today, so I put on a Fendi t-shirt, a pair of jean shorts I had cut up myself, and Fendi sneakers.

"We ready, heffa. Ooh, well don't you look fine. I like the bun," Shanice complimented. "Now I feel like I'm doing too much." I looked at her fitted dress and Balenciaga sneakers and disagreed.

"No, boo, you looking thick, thick. Now this bitch right here," I pointed to Mecca who had on a pair of jean shorts like me, but she paired hers with a bralette and wedge sandals. "*She's* doing too much. Mecca, you know there's gonna be kids at the park, right?" She was damn near naked.

"Girl, I know, I'm putting on a blazer." I shook my head at her extra ass.

My parents had gone away for the week, so I was able to leave the house without the third degree about how short my shorts were. We hopped in my car and made our way Uptown. I didn't want to bother Maine by texting him that I was en route. I figured he'd be busy getting ready for his performance anyway. He'd practice a few times in front of me at his house, and I'd assured him that he was ready, but he was a perfectionist. I appreciated that quality in him. When we arrived, the park was packed out. Ant had really done his big one.

Food trucks were set up and a bunch of activities for the kids that came out. It was such a good time when black people came together for a good cause. We could hear the music before we fully entered the park, the DJ had it rockin'. Spotting my sister and Heaven under a tent close to the stage, I signaled for the girls to follow me to them.

"Hey sissy, I was wondering when you were gonna get here." She hugged and kissed my cheek and did the same with the girls.

"You know getting this fine takes time, sis," I joked and slapped fives with her. Giving Heaven the same hug and kiss, we sat down in the chairs that were reserved for us. "Have you seen Maine? Is he nervous?"

"Look at her, all concerned about her man. Yes, boo, young A Boogie just walked inside the center with Ant,"

Heaven said, smiling at me. Just then, I spotted him across the park talking to Kandice. It didn't look like a friendly conversation either. I wanted to watch how it played out, but something told me she was overstepping her boundaries and an ass whipping was overdue.

"What you wanna do?" Mecca asked, down for whatever as always. I looked to Kris and she nodded, silently giving me the go head. She was the more levelheaded of us two. While she could take a lot, I had little to no patience. Whereas it took a minute for her to go off, I was on yo' ass in two point five if I felt disrespected. I walked over by myself, knowing that my girls would show they ass if they tagged along.

"Hey, babe," I interrupted their conversation. Maine didn't jump or give me any sign that he was on bullshit and that was a good thing.

"Wassup, beautiful?" He responded, kissing my lips, placing his hands around my waist, and sliding me in front of him.

"Oh word, Maine? You sure you wanna do this?" She low-key threatened with her hand on her hip. I felt my body getting hot, but I wouldn't let her see me sweat. I wanted to know what she was talking about. In her face Maine and I would be a united front.

"Go 'head with that bullshit you talking, I already told you what it is." He waved her off and grabbed me by the hand so that we could walk away.

"No problem, we'll just handle up on it in the next few

months then." Instinctively, I squeezed his hand, but my facial expression didn't change.

"Stop talking in riddles and say what you gotta say," I pressed, knowing the next thing that came from her mouth wasn't going to be anything I wanted to hear.

"From now on, I'll only address my baby daddy. You're a non motherfucking factor." She smiled deviously before waving and walking away. It took everything in me not to run behind her and snatch her ass up. *Pregnant? How the fuck could she be pregnant when I was pregnant?*

Kristen

I watched from afar as my sister approached Maine and silently hoped that nothing popped off. Ant had worked tirelessly at putting this event together and I didn't want it to be ruined. I mean, I was gonna be right beside my sister if anything popped off, I was just crossing my fingers that it wouldn't come to that.

"Bitch," Heaven nudged me in my side, making me scowl at her. "Look at Kane's ass over there with China." I didn't want to, but I looked anyway. He was standing near her at one of the food trucks, surveying the area. This wasn't even his type of scene, so I had no clue why he was here, nor did I care.

"Fuck Kane. Come on y'all, lets go in the crowd so we can watch Maine do his thang." The girls followed me, and we met Kaia at the front of the stage. "Everything okay?" I inquired, checking for any signs of brewing beef.

"We good," she stated simply. I wanted to say more but thought better of it. The beat dropped to Maine's single "The One" and the crowd went crazy reciting the chorus.

Shorty, you the one, yeah shorty, you the one. You just tell me what to do and a nigga get it done. Shorty, you the one, yeah shorty, you the one. You just tell me what to do and a nigga get it done.

He commanded the crowd, both men and women with his stage presence. My eyes lingered to the corner of the stage where Ant was. He had a proud smile on his face as Maine performed. I knew he was so proud of his brother. While I gazed at him, I felt a pair of eyes burning a hole in my face. Regretfully, I looked in that direction and there Kane was not even hiding the fact that he was lusting after me.

I ignored him and went back to cheering Maine on. After his performance, the talent show started. I had to admit a lot of the people had skills. I'd hate to be in Antwon's shoes, having to sort through all that talent was going to be a lot. Once all of the acts had their time, the DJ kept the party going and the girls and I retired back to the section set up for us. Kaia was still acting a little off, so I excused myself and pulled her off to the side with me.

"Okay, wassup? You've been spacey since coming back from the little pow wow with Maine and ol' girl."

"I'm fine, Kris." She looked down at her feet and started to fidget. Right then, I knew she was lying.

"Kaia, look at me," I demanded. When she finally did, her eyes had swelled up and tears pooled in the corners. "Oh my God, sissy, tell me what's wrong." I wanted to pull her in my arms but didn't want the girls to think something was wrong, so I grabbed her hand instead.

"Kandice is pregnant." Well shit, I didn't expect that. I was about to respond but stopped because she had more news. "I am, too."

"I'm sorry, come again?" I needed her to repeat that shit for me.

"I'm pregnant, Kristen," she repeated with her head down again.

"Oh God, Kaia! Nooo, Stink. You have ya whole life ahead of you. Shit." This time I said fuck what the girls may do. I pulled her into me and hugged her tight. My baby sister was just eighteen. She didn't need a baby right now, she had dreams. I wanted to kick Maine's ass. Then again, I couldn't blame him, I knew the sex was consensual. "It's okay, I got you. We got this," I assured her. I helped her get herself together and we headed back to our circle.

Feeling someone pull at my hand, I spun around and bumped into Kane. He took advantage of the moment and held me by my arms. Snatching away quickly, I went to walk away, but he pulled me back, roughly.

"Get ya fucking hands off me!" I spoke through tight lips. I was so over this bullshit with Kane's punk ass.

"You got with Ant and now you gangsta? I can't even fucking talk to you, Kristen?!"

"No, you cannot. What part of fuck off don't you understand? Now get ya hands off me before I..."

"Before you what? You know what I'm capable of, so don't threaten me, Kristen." He gave me a hard glare and squeezed my arm tighter. With Kaia having walked a few steps ahead of me, we somehow got split up amongst the crowd of people, so I was on my own.

"Detective Kane, you have five seconds to unhand my woman before the NYPD be saying their goodbyes to their fellow officer," Antwon threatened behind him, causing Kane to release his grip on my arm. Soon as he did, Antwon hit him with a mean right hook, making him fall. "Fuck is yo' problem putting yo' hands on a woman and *my* woman at that?" Antwon had a look in his eyes that I had never seen. It was almost as if he was a different person. A small crowd started to form, and the girls and Maine had come over.

I couldn't take Ant going to jail for defending me, so I grabbed at his hand to pull him away, but he stayed planted. "He's not worth it, babe, let's go." I pulled at him again, only a little harder. This time he complied.

"How you know Kane, Kristen?" He hadn't called me by my first name since meeting me, so I took it as a sign that he was upset.

"Umm, he's my ex," I spilled.

"Hol' up, *that's* the nigga who used to put his fucking hands on you and put you in the fucking hospital?!" He roared, causing people to divert their attention to us.

"Calm yo' ass down, bringing all this attention to us," I whispered harshly. I didn't need a whole bunch of people all in my business. "Can we talk about this at another time?" He shook his head and walked off, leaving me standing there in my feelings.

"Come on, girl, it's okay. Let's go to my house. You and Kaia looking all sad and shit, we not gonna be able to enjoy the rest of the festivities." Heaven hugged me and I agreed. Antwon had hurt my feelings with his reaction. I had broken down and told him about my past with my ex and the abuse. I purposely left out Kane's name as well as his occupation. I didn't think I'd see him here and I damn sure wouldn't have guessed that Antwon knew him.

I had driven with Heaven, so we headed to her car while Kaia and the girls went in hers. I let them know to meet me at my house instead, I needed a strong drink. I didn't even bother telling Antwon that I was leaving. He was being an asshole about the situation, and I wasn't feeling him at the moment. As we drove, I got a call from one of my stylists, Mia.

"Hey Mia, wassup?"

"Kristen, get to the shop right now, right now!" She exclaimed, causing me to be on high alert.

"Wha...what's going on, Mia?" I don't know why but my stomach started to tighten. In my heart, I knew there was something wrong.

"Kristen, please just get down here to the shop asap," she pleaded before hanging up on me.

"Heaven, turn the car around, we gotta get to the shop." She looked like she wanted to ask questions, but I'm glad she didn't because I didn't have any answers.

WHEN WE PULLED UP, I thought my eyes were deceiving me. There were two fire trucks outside, along with police cars and a crowd that seemed to be growing. I felt weak as I stepped out of the car onto the pavement. My feet felt like boulders as I moved towards the front of my shop where firemen were walking out. Mia spotted me before I could make it through the crowd and ran towards me with outstretched arms.

"Kristen, wait, you don't wanna go over there," she spoke through tear-filled eyes. By now, Heaven had caught up to me and clasped her hand in mine.

"I gotta see it." I let her hand go and pushed my way through the sea of people with them both on my heels. I made it to the front, only to collapse to the ground when I saw the state of what used to be my shop. "Nooooo!" I screamed until I felt my throat go dry. Someone had set fire to my place. All that could be seen was the remnants of it through the smoke as the firemen cleared it out.

"I got you, cousin, it's gonna be alright." Heaven did her best to console me as she lifted me from the ground. I was inconsolable as I watched my livelihood turn into charcoal. I cried so hard that my body shook. She hugged me tightly and rubbed my back in a circular motion and although it did nothing to ease the pain I felt, it did calm me down a little.

"Why would someone do this shit to me, Heaven? I'm a good fucking person!" My voice held so much pain and despair, I didn't know what to do.

"Ma'am, are you the owner of this establishment?" A detective who looked like she'd rather be elsewhere inquired.

"Yes, she is. Can you tell us about what happened here?" Heaven spoke for me. Out of the two of us she was the most composed, even though I knew this shit was eating her up, too.

"I need to speak with the owner."

"Are you fucking kidding me? I said she's right here. Clearly, you see that she's in distress right now. You know what? Get the fuck away from us and find us a supervisor to talk to." Heaven flipped and I knew I had to step in.

"Can you just tell me what happened, detective? As she stated, I'm the owner, Kristen Phillips."

She gave Heaven a nasty look before she speaking again. "Well, it looks like a case of arson. The perpetrator broke into the establishment, poured gasoline throughout different parts of the shop, and sparked the fire."

"This bitch," Heaven scoffed. "We know it was arson, Captain Obvious." The officer looked like she was gearing up to go at Heaven but decided against it.

"I have a couple questions for you, Ms. Phillips. Do you think you can come down to the station?"

"Right now, I'm not in the right state of mind. If you give me your card, I'll have my lawyer be in touch." I knew it wasn't the answer she was looking for, but right now I could give a fuck. She worked for the same precinct Kane did. I could tell by her badge. She handed me her card and I took one last look at my shop before walking away. "This got Kane written all over it," I said to Heaven once we were back in the car.

I thought back to the day I was at Antwon's house and wouldn't respond to his anonymous calls or texts. He had mentioned the shop and now he had found a fucked-up way to get my attention. This motherfucka had awakened something in me so vicious, I was gonna make sure he wished he'd never met me.

I texted Kaia, letting her know I was on my way home and there was an emergency. I wanted her to drop the girls before I got there. Heaven and I rode in silence to my place, no music or anything, just our own thoughts. Reclining my seat back, I put my hand over my face and cried. Kane knew what he was doing when he torched my shop. He was trying to break me, but one thing about God's children, we may bend but we didn't break.

Ant

For the past week, I had immersed myself in work to keep my mind off of what happened at my event with Kristen. We were barely speaking now outside of little meaningless texts here and there. That shit wasn't nobody's fault, but mine. After finding out that Detective Kane was the ex she had cried to me about, I was heated. This bitch made nigga had put his fucking hands on my woman and was still living to talk about it. Granted, I hadn't known her at the time, but it didn't matter, I knew her now.

"Yo', you need to call, Kristen. You been stuck in this office since shit went left at the event," Maine's irritating ass said, walking into my office without knocking.

"Do you need something?" I was annoyed with him telling me the same damn thing.

"Yeah, I need my woman, but she ain't fucking with a nigga right now. You, on the other hand, ain't going through it near as bad as me." He was right, that baby situation took the cake.

"Wassup with you and that situation, man?" I changed the subject to get him to acknowledge his own damn problems.

"Man, Kandice is a stupid ass broad. She know damn well she ain't pregnant with my seed. And what's even more fucked up is that Kaia won't even answer the phone to let me explain." He was just as stressed as me. I was taken back by his reaction, though. This was the same person who didn't have time for love a couple months ago. "What? Why you looking at me like that?"

I chuckled. "Nothing, it's good to see you growing up." I smiled like a proud dad.

"Nigga, grow up these nuts. Let's go across the street to the Big House." The Big House was what I named the studio at Promise Records. It was across the street from the main building and was used for recording and rehearsal only.

"Invite me to ya nuts again and we gon' have a problem, my boy."

"That was disrespectful, huh?" He snickered.

"Yeah aight, keep playing." I grabbed my phone and hoody to go across the way. Stopping short, I picked up my ringing phone. When Chloe's voice came through, I immediately regretted the decision.

"Hey, can you come get Bre? I'm getting ready to go on a date. He should be here in a few." Stunned by her calm demeanor, I looked at the caller ID to make sure it was Chloe I was talking to.

"Chloe?"

"Yeah, who else would it be?" She answered, still calm as ever. I silently thanked God for small miracles and let her know I'd be there in twenty minutes. "Yo' ride with me to pick up Bre and then I wanna swing by Kristen's real quick." He agreed and hopped in my car.

"Yo' shorty, you got me fucked up if you think you gon' keep ignoring my calls like I'm some lame ass nigga. You better call me back before I do something crazy," Maine threatened into his phone before hanging up. I cracked up laughing when he threw the phone on the dashboard. I laughed all the way to Chloe's house.

"Don't worry, lil' bro, we getting our women back today. You waiting here or you coming up?" We had parked in front of her building. I wanted to be in and out.

"Nah, I'll wait down here but hurry up."

"Aight, Keith Sweat, let me leave you to beg in peace." I got out and closed the door. Unlike the last time I popped up, I didn't use my key. She had some sense on the phone, so I knocked instead.

"Who is it?" Bre's little voice said through the door.

"It's the daddy that's gonna beat ya little butt for being at this door. Go get mommy, Breann." I was really raising a grown little adult. Chloe opened the door a few seconds later all dressed up.

Stepping back, to let me walk inside, she put her hand up. "Before you go questioning my parenting skills, I was in the bathroom and didn't know she went to the door." I cut my eyes at Bree who was pouting.

"Sorry daddy." I tried to remain serious but failed. She was daddy's baby. I picked her up in my arms and kissed her cheek.

"It's okay, princess. Don't do that again, though." I put her down and she ran off to her room. "You look really nice," I complimented Chloe. The red spandex dress fit her in all the right places. I made sure not to look too hard.

"Thank you. That little girl of yours is a piece of work, you know that, right?" I chuckled and nodded in agreement. There was a knock on the door, and I looked at her to see if she was going to go and answer it. "Oh, can you get that for me? I need to finish getting myself together." She just kept shocking me, but I didn't object. I wanted to meet this dude.

Now if God was the man like I knew him to be, he'd keep Chloe in this pleasant space. Taking out my phone to text Kristen, I let her know I wanted to see her so we could talk.

Wifey: *I can't make any promises, I'm busy today.*

She hit me with a hard curve, but there was no point in

responding. I was gonna take my chances and pop up anyway.

"Ant, get the door!" Chloe shouted from the back.

"I am. This nigga ain't the president, he can wait!" I yelled back. I knew the comment pissed her off. Opening the door and seeing Detective Kane standing in front of me, I didn't know whether to close it or knock this nigga in his head again. "Fuck you doing here?"

"Umm, hey, Kane," Chloe spoke, pushing me back from the door a little and allowing him to step in. "This is my daughter's father, Ant. Ant, this is Kane, my date." He stuck out his hand to shake mine and I took it as him trying to be funny.

"Nigga, don't make me break ya fucking jaw."

"Really, Ant?"

"Ay man, I don't have no problems with you and sorry about what happened at the park with Kristen. I didn't know y'all was together."

"Yeah aight." I turned my head to Chloe. "Just so you know, this nigga likes to beat his women, so you think about that while you out on your date. Bre, come on mamas." Bre's little feet could be heard running to the front. She had her little purse on her arm, and we left out without me saying another word to Chloe or Kane.

As we approached the car, I could hear Maine beefing on the phone, but I was too caught up in my own thoughts.

Strapping Bre in her car seat, I got in and sped off. Kane possibly dating my baby's mom and doing her like he did Kristen had me going. The only difference was, Chloe wasn't letting me stop shit in her life. All I know was she had better keep the nigga away from my daughter or I was sure to pop his ass, cop or not.

I wanted to drop Bre off to my mom before I headed over to Kris's house, but I figured with her with me, Kris wouldn't close the door in my face. I was missing my girl and the fact that she had just as much, if not more, pride than me, I knew I had met my match. Helping Bre out the car, we walked into Kris's building. I gave the doorman a head nod and we stepped into the elevator.

"Daddy, where we going?"

"To see my friend real quick, then I'ma take you to the park."

"Okay. Uncle Maine you coming, too?"

"Nah, I got things to do lil' mama," he crushed her little dreams. Her bottom lip poked out and Maine smiled. "Toughen up, gangsta baby, I'm coming." Bre jumped up and down, excited that she would be able to run the both of us ragged at the park. At Kris's door, I knocked hard and no one answered. Not believing she wasn't home, I knocked again, this time harder than the last.

"Who is it?" Kaia's voice made Maine stand up straight from where he leaned against the door.

"It's Bre," Bre answered, making me and Maine laugh.

Good thing it got Kaia to open the door. When she saw us, I'm sure she wanted to close it, but seeing Bre's big dough eyes made her think twice.

"Can we come in?" I asked and she opened the door, allowing us entry.

Kaia

The last thing I expected was to see Maine and the crew at my sister's door. I had to focus on the little girl that stood in between him and Ant to prevent my heart from skipping a beat the way it did when I first opened the door. I bent down eye level with the little beauty who wasn't shy at all. She didn't cower behind her dad's leg, she stayed planted in front with her little Gucci purse hanging off her arm.

"Hey pretty girl, who are you here for?"

"My daddy's friend. What her name, daddy?" She looked up at Ant and he smirked.

"Kristen, baby girl."

"Her name, Kristen baby girl. Is she here?" We all shared a laugh at how serious her face was. I stepped backed and they walked in.

"Kaia, who's at the door?" Kris asked as she came into view in a pair of biker shorts and bra less under her wife beater. "Oh, dammit," she ran back to her room to get decent.

"Can we talk?" Maine spoke. I had yet to acknowledge his presence.

"Nope. I wanna hang with little pretty," I said, referring to who I'd come to know as Bre, Ant's daughter.

"Man, bring yo' ass out here in this hallway and talk to me. I'm done with this shit with you." Maine grabbed my hand, causing Bre to look at him. "Sorry, Bre, I'll give you some money later." He pulled me towards the door, and I moved in the opposite direction where the balcony was.

"We can talk back here. And stop pulling on me like you crazy." He followed me and once we made it out to the balcony, I closed the door behind us. "Talk," I said with my arms crossed.

He swiped his hand over his face and let out a long sigh. "Look, this shit is crazy, man. I've been missing yo' ass and you been hiding from me. And over some bullshit. Kandice is *not* carrying my damn baby. I strapped up every time with that broad. Who you gon' believe her or your man?"

"The DNA test."

"I'll take that shit, that's no problem. It's just gonna prove what I already said."

"Okay, you done?"

"Yo', you deadass?" His face held an annoyed and angry expression. I wanted to hug him so bad, kiss his face, and tell him how much I missed him, but my pride wouldn't let me. "I'm pregnant too, Tremaine," I blurted out the secret I'd been keeping from him.

"Huh?" He responded, dumbfounded.

"Man, move, you heard what I said." I went to push past him to go back inside, but he grabbed me by my waist.

"Hold on, shorty, wait." He nuzzled my neck and held me tight. "You pregnant with my baby?" Him saying it caused all kinds of emotions to pour out of me as I started to tear up.

"I am, but I can't keep the baby, Tremaine." Instead of pulling away from me he held me tighter. I wasn't scared of how he would react when I told him, but this wasn't what I expected.

"I understand, shorty. Can I at least be there when you do the procedure?" I turned around to face him and his eyes were sincere, and they also held a bit of sadness.

"I love you." For the first time, I expressed what I'd been feeling for a while now. I didn't care about what his response would be. Right now, in this moment, I wanted him to know how I felt.

"I love you, too." He held my face in his hands and kissed my lips sensually. My body heated up quickly and I squealed once I felt his hands palm my booty. We continued tongue wrestling until his phone went off. I was able to peek at the caller ID when he pulled it from his pocket. It was Kandice calling and I was mad all over again.

"You might as well answer it." I didn't want to hear the conversation, so I went to walk away. Again, he pulled me back and put the phone on speaker for me to hear.

"Yo'."

"Maine, I need some money," her voice came through, irking my soul.

"What you telling me that for?" Shit, even I wanted to know the answer to that.

"Because I wanna go shopping for the baby."

"Then you should call the baby's father."

"Stop playing with me, Maine. I'm on the phone with my child's father."

"Nah, you're on the phone with a father of a child, just not yours."

"So, what you saying?" The whole conversation was pissing me off because she couldn't get a clue. I snatched the phone to help.

"He's saying, we'll see you in a few months for a DNA test, dummy. Now get off this line begging." I hung up, handed him back the phone, and went back inside the house. Going into the living room, I found my sister, Ant, and his daughter sitting on the couch watching the black version of *Annie*. They looked so cute and I didn't want to interrupt their family moment, so I decided to head home.

"Y'all look real cozy, so I'm gonna head out."

"Aww okay, sis. Thank you for being here for me."

"Girl, stop acting dumb, that's my job. And don't worry about the shop, it'll be back up and running in no time." She motioned with her hand for me to shut up, but I already spilled the beans. Shit, how was I supposed to know she hadn't told Ant yet?

"What happened with the shop?"

"Kane's punk ass set fire to it or paid somebody to do it." I looked towards the door where Heaven casually walked in with a bag from Red Lobster. She just blurted that shit out of nowhere, we hadn't even heard her come in.

"His punk ass did **what?!**" Ant's voice boomed while Maine pulled out his phone and began typing really fast.

"You do see Bre right there, right?" Kris mentioned. Bre's eyes were wide as saucers, all in our conversation. I didn't laugh because I didn't want her to think it was okay, but that shit was funny as hell. "I'll explain later, let me take Kaia home real quick."

"I got her, sis," Maine offered, and Ant tossed him his keys. Heaven came out and hugged me like it was normal for her to just walk into people's house.

"How's Rel and Kelsey?" I asked Maine as he drove.

"They're good, back with their mother. She surprised me when she completed the program. It was hard giving them back to her, but it's her responsibility to be their parent."

"And what do you think about being a parent?" I don't know what made me ask since I had already made up my mind that I couldn't have the baby. I wanted to know how he felt, though.

"Honestly, after having Rel and Kels for a little while, I got used to them being around. I think I'd be a great father. We'd make a pretty baby, too." I smiled big. I wasn't too far along so I wasn't attached to the baby, but I couldn't lie and say that I wasn't attached to the thought of being a mom. Before I could say anything else, I noticed the red, blue, and white flashing lights and the sirens soon followed. I tensed up, but Maine remained calm. "It's cool, baby, calm down." He held my hand and that soothed me a little. He pulled over and the cop didn't get out immediately. That was a red flag for me. I knew we weren't speeding, and we hadn't run any lights so what the hell was going on? After a few minutes, the cop finally got out and headed our way.

"Good evening, license and registration?" He directed his questioning towards Maine. I wanted to record the interaction but was too scared to let go of Maine's hand.

"I'ma reach over and hand you the registration and grab my license from my wallet. Can you tell us why you pulled us over?" Maine asked with one hand on the steering wheel and the other I held hostage in my lap. I let his hand go so that he could get the items.

"We suspect that drugs are being transported in this vehicle. Stay put while I run your information." The cop walked away, and I looked to Maine. He squeezed my hand, reassuring me that we would be okay. When the cop came back, he demanded that we step out of the car.

"Let's just get out, bae. We know there's nothing in here," I said to him. I knew him nor Ant were dumb enough to carry anything on them, so I wasn't worried about that. He agreed and we got out. We were told to stand on the side of the car with our hands above our heads. All the while I kept thinking, who would have reported this *specific* car as having drugs in it? The shit just didn't make sense. I could feel flutters in my stomach, and I knew I was way too early in the pregnancy to feel anything from the little tadpole I was carrying. I was nervous as hell.

When the search was done, he stood in front of us with a paper bag in his hand. He opened it and tilted it towards Maine, so only he was able to see the contents inside. Maine's face remained neutral as the cop closed the bag.

"Tremaine Brown, you are under arrest for conspiring to transport cocaine." I went numb as the officer mirandized Maine and handcuffed him.

"Kaia, Kaia," I heard him call out to me, snapping me back into reality. "Baby, drive the car back to your sister's crib and tell Ant what happened. He'll know what to do." The tears leaked from my eyes as I watched him be shoved into the police car. "Bae, do what I said!" He yelled out. The police car drove off and I immediately snapped into action. Jumping in the driver's seat, I turned the car around and headed back to Kris's house. I didn't even bother calling.

I must've hit ninety on the highway because I got to my sister's house in under fifteen minutes. Parking the car quickly, I disregarded the door man, ran into the open elevator, and pressed Kris's floor. I paced back and forth, wondering how the fuck drugs got into the car and why the cop only took Maine and not me. Soon as the elevator dinged on Kris's floor, I ran to her door and opened it.

"Antwon, the police arrested Maine."

"What?!" He yelled out, before running over to where I was, standing up against the door. I told him what happened, and he rushed out the door, completely forgetting that he'd left Bre behind.

"Are you okay?" Both Heaven and Kris asked as I started to hyperventilate.

"Kris, you go over there with Bre. Let me handle her," Heaven suggested. She took me into the kitchen and sat me down. "Alright Kaia, come on, boo, you gotta calm down. Here, drink this water." I drunk the water she gave me and took a deep breath to get myself together.

"I need him, Heaven. I...I need him." She hugged me and I cried on her shoulder.

Maine

Detective Kane was playing dirty. I already knew his ass was behind the bogus ass stop as soon as I was handcuffed. I hated that Kaia had to witness me being shoved into the back of a police car. She looked so distraught and I needed her to hold it down at least until she got to Ant. Finding out she was carrying my baby put a lot of shit into perspective for me, even though she wasn't trying to keep it. And even though I didn't want her to get rid of it, I knew I had to support her decision. We both had our whole lives ahead of us. I was able to say that confidently because I knew I was getting out of this shit.

"Mr. Brown, you gotta give us something so we can let

you go. We know you're an up-and-coming rap star and all that shit so this can't be yo' coke we found in the trunk."

"Lawyer."

These pigs had the game fucked up if they thought I had anything else to say other than that. I sat back in the wobbly chair with my arms folded across my chest and got comfortable. For their sake and mine, I hoped they wouldn't start no good cop, bad cop bullshit because the first dude to jump in my face, I was rocking his shit. The detective stood up from where he was leaned in on the table and walked out of the room. Minutes later, my lawyer, Jeffrey Klein, walked in. Jeffrey was a smooth-talking beast when it came to the courtroom.

"Hey, this shit is not looking good." That wasn't what I wanted to hear.

"What you mean, Jeff?"

"Man, they're holding you without bond. This precinct is under investigation for corruption, so the Captain is playing by the book."

"You call some shit being planted in Ant's car by the book, Jeff? Get the fuck outta here, man! When I'm getting outta this shit?" I raised my voice because this whole thing was pissing me the fuck off.

"I'm working on it, man, trust me. You know I always come through."

"You better. And yo', get with my brother, he knows who's behind this shit." As if on cue a cop came in and told me to stand up. Next thing I knew, I was being tossed my orange jump suit. *Ain't this about a bitch.*

IT HAD BEEN six months since the bogus ass arrest, and I was locked up on Rikers Island. I was still fucked up as to how they were able to keep me for so long on this bullshit. According to Jeff, they had yet to officially charge me and he had been going back and forth with the DA for months on the matter. Ant had been holding me down of course and coming to see me weekly. He had yet to catch up with Kane, though.

According to Chloe, who I found out was dating him, she hadn't seen him in months. I didn't think she was lying because she didn't want problems with Ant. I hadn't seen Kaia because I didn't want her to see me behind these walls. I did make sure that we spoke on the phone every day. She was in my corner and it kept me going, knowing that she was holding shit down. Six months may have felt like nothing to someone on the outside, but in here, that shit seemed like forever.

"Brown, visit," a guard called out to me. I was in my cell, staring at the ceiling. Something I did often. I wasn't trying to get cool with none of the grimy niggas in here. Entering the visiting room, I spotted Ant sitting with Rel at a table in the corner. *The hell was he doing bringing him here?* I thought to myself.

"Before you go wildin', just know the lil' nigga hopped in my car and wouldn't move until I agreed to let him come up here with me," Ant said while dapping me up. I did the same with Rel.

"I had to come see you. I wanted to tell y'all what I found out about who popped at y'all at that club a while back." So much had gone on in between the night at the club and when I got locked up, we had put that on the back burner. I was all ears by now and by the way Ant's face was all twisted up, he was too. "Kareem did that shit at the guidance of Detective Kane."

"Who told you that, bro?" This nigga had his hands in everything fucked up that was going on with us.

"I overheard some dudes talking about it outside of Al's store on 40th a couple days ago. They were talking about how Reem had did that shit to get back at you for stopping him from being on the block." I had my suspicions about Kareem being behind the shooting but never put too much into confirming it.

"I know all this shit is about me being with Kristen, bruh," Ant confirmed what we both already knew. "I'm on this nigga's head as soon as he comes out of hiding." I nodded and changed the subject. I didn't want to dwell on what had already been confirmed. I needed out of this bitch asap. We sat and chopped it up about what was going on at the record label. Bro had signed three more dope artists and my mixtape was still getting heavy rotation on several platforms, even on the radio.

After visiting hours were up, I retired back to my six by eight feet cell with my Spanish cellie who spoke broken English. I laid back on my bunk, thinking about Kaia and our baby. Whenever we spoke on the phone, she never mentioned whether or not she got the abortion. She would just pass on the conversation altogether. What I did know was that Kandice had indeed had her baby and from what my brother told me, he looked a lot like me. If that baby was mine, I knew for a fact that the bitch had poked a hole in the condom when I wasn't looking. Probably with her teeth when she opened it. I didn't put nothing past her scandalous ass.

The day dragged like it had done for the past six months. The jail shit was for the birds. I couldn't understand how niggas were in and out of here like they got paid to do it. Tired of laying down, I headed to the rec area and went straight for the weight bar to do some pull ups. Mid pull up, I spotted a nigga that looked like Kareem on the basketball court. Well, I'd be damned if it wasn't him playing ball and talking shit. I was a one-man army in here and I didn't know what kind of connections he had so I wasn't going to approach him on the yard, but he would see me.

"Yo' Maine," I turned in the direction my name was being called and spotted my boy Dino walking into the yard.

"My nigga, what you doing here? You supposed to be on the streets," I spoke to him while giving him dap.

"Nigga, I got cased up. Ant ain't tell you they came and swept up the blocks?" I looked at him with a raised brow.

"Yeah man, the cops playing dirty, thanks to Reem's talking ass," he spat with a scowl on his face.

"You mean *that* Reem over there?" I pointed to Kareem on the basketball court.

"Oh, I'ma 'bout to go poke this nigga up. He got us *all* jammed up on this bullshit." I put my hand on his chest to stop him.

"We gon' get his ass, but a different way. He don't think I know about him shooting at us in the club, but it's confirmed. I'ma get you something and we gon' get that taken care of." He nodded and we walked off in the opposite direction. It was always a snake in the grass.

I needed to hear Kaia's voice, so I headed for the phones. Picking up the state phone, I wiped it off before dialing. She accepted the charges immediately and my heart thumped when her voice came through the speakers.

"Hey, baby," she cooed into the phone.

"Wassup, shorty? How you doing?"

She sighed before answering,. **"I'd be better if you were here, but we're doing good."** I picked up on the *we* part of her answer immediately.

"Who's we?"

"Oh, me and Kris," she said quickly. **"You know ya**

brother has been stressing about you being down. We've been keeping each other's spirits up." I nodded as if she could see me and rubbed the fuzz that was growing on my chin. "Babe, you there?"

"Yeah, I'm here. I miss you, shorty."

"I miss you too, Tremaine. I miss you so much."

I could hear her sniffling and the last thing I wanted to do was make her cry. I changed the subject to something more joyous. She had been sketching a lot lately and was sending swatches to different companies to get her designs put on runways and shit like that. That kind of talk usually brightened her spirits. We spoke for a few more minutes before the automated voice stated the call was ending. After exchanging I love you's, we hung up.

I'd be better if you were here, but we're doing good. That statement stayed with me as I slept. There was something Kaia wasn't telling me, but I'd find out soon enough.

THE NEXT MORNING, I got up with a plan to take care of Reem. I tapped the side of my bunk to get the attention of my cellie.

"Me puedes conseguir algo?" (Can you get me something?)

"Que necesitas?" (What do you need?)

"Una herramienta." (A tool) The only people who knew I spoke Spanish fluently was my mom and brother. Ant knew his way around the language as well. He always said it was important to at least know Spanish, so when motherfuckas spoke about you in their language, you'd know. The cellie jumped down from the top bunk and handed me a makeshift knife.

"One hundred dollars, my friend," he said, referring to the payment he wanted for the tool. His English was just as clear as mine was about that paper.

"It'll be on your books before the end of the day." I secured the knife in my pants and walked down to the first tier where Dino was housed and passed it off to him. I nodded towards the showers and his face showed that he understood what I was telling him without speaking. I stood over in the area of the showers and Dino showed up with Reem a few minutes later.

"Yo' Dino, I ain't with that gay shit my nigga, wassup?" I heard Reem talking shit.

"Don't play with me like that, my nigga. I just wanted to politic with you for a minute." I was in a blind spot so he couldn't see me. "You out here turning Fed after I put you on, dawg?"

"I don't know what you talking bout, my nigga." He couldn't look Dino in the eye and that confirmed what we already knew.

"So, the streets is lying? You ain't get with that detective about our operation? You ain't get Maine tripped up on some fraud shit?"

"Dawg, fuck Maine! That's why yo' ass in here cause you too busy dick riding. That nigga ain't God, bro."

"You right," I rounded the corner and his eyes got bigger. "I ain't God, he's the one that gave you life. I'ma be the nigga to take it." I motioned to Dino and he stuck him in the neck, making sure to get his jugular.

Cleaning off the knife, we walked out the same way we came in. Rikers didn't give a fuck about the inmates so there would be no investigation. One rat down, one pig to go.

Kristen

The last few months had been trying to say the least. Between trying to get my shop back in order and being there for Ant, I didn't know whether I was coming or going. Don't get me wrong, I didn't mind being there for my man at all. It was just a lot to juggle. He had been bringing Bre around more as well. Of course, her mother wasn't feeling it, but I made it a point to let her know I wasn't trying to take her spot in her daughter's life. If anything, I was hoping to add to it.

I would say the good thing about this whole ordeal was Ant being able to hang up the streets and focus on the record company. It was more involuntary than voluntary. His blocks in Harlem were raided weeks after Maine was locked up. Again, the work of Kane, I'm sure. He hadn't been harassing me since finding my shop burnt up. Remember when I mentioned my own payback?

Well let's just say that I sent in pictures of my many bruises as well as me laid up in the hospital the last time he knocked me out. I made sure to send the pictures anonymously. Knowing there was all kinds of corruption going on within the precinct he worked in, I didn't know what would be done with the pictures. Good thing Kaia made sure I gave a copy to both her and Heaven. If anything were to happen to me, they would send them to every news outlet.

I had to really build my business from the ground up. Thank God for the insurance I had on the shop, so all of the damage was covered. Mrs. Thomas was even gracious enough to give me the building. After everything that happened, she said it was the least she could do. I was so grateful to her and her caring heart. Although the fire had taken the memories, I wouldn't let it break my spirit or the people who helped me make my dream a reality.

Tonight, I wanted a quiet night to love on my man. I'd called him earlier in the day and let him know I was taking him out. With the new artists he signed, he was so busy at work dealing with A&R's, contracts, studio sessions, etc. My baby deserved a break. I didn't think that I'd find love like what I had with Ant after coming out of my hell with Kane.

Antwon was different and I thanked his mom every day

for making him for me. She, Kaia, and I had become pretty close in the past couple months. Kaia made Ma Jane's her home when she wasn't home being catered to by my mom. They both loved the back and forth and didn't complain. Before heading to meet with Ant, I needed to stop by the shop to pick up the spare key to give to Heaven. Using my key to enter the shop, I didn't get to fully open the door before I was hit from behind. The blow didn't knock me out, but it did daze me, causing me to stumble and fall. Before I could get my bearings, I felt myself being dragged by my hair.

"Let me go!" I tried to fight back and loosen the person's grip from my curls. Thrown into the wall, I felt a sharp pain shoot up my spine. I knew my back had hit the wood that lined the wall. "Ouch!" I yelped in intense pain.

"Shut up, bitch!" I recognized the voice as China's but didn't point it out.

"Aye, watch that shit!" I jumped when I heard Kane's.

Why can't this bastard just leave me alone? I said to myself.

"Okay, so what we gon' do now?" Another female spoke, whose voice I couldn't place. The shop was pitch black and seeing that it was nine in the evening, in the middle of winter, it was dark outside as well. I couldn't make out any faces because Kane was smart enough to make sure his entourage had on black also.

"Why did you bring her anyway, Kane? I swear it's like every stray you find, you have to bring them home," China argued.

"Oh, I got ya stray bitch," the other woman retorted. As they argued, I mustered all my strength and attempted to crawl towards the door. "Where you think you going?" The woman sent a fierce kick to my side and I swore I heard my rib crack.

"Kaneeeee!" I screamed out to him in pain, shocking myself. If I knew anything, I knew he wouldn't want me to be hurt by anyone else's hands but his.

"Chloe, what the fuck is your problem?!" He barked before bending down to pick me up gently. This man was sick. "Go to the car, we've been here too long already."

"You serious, Kane? Let that bitch walk."

"China, if you and Chloe don't get to the car, I'ma put my foot in y'all ass." That got her to moving.

"This some bullshit," China mumbled under her breath before removing her hoodie.

The name Chloe ring in my head and I just knew it wasn't the same *Chloe* I was thinking of. My suspicions were confirmed once she removed her hoody as well. My blood boiled at the sight of Ant's baby mother. I watched as she grabbed my purse from the floor and went through it, retrieving my phone before throwing my bag back down. Kane placed me gently in the back of a black van and whispered he loved me in my ear. I felt my skin crawl. This couldn't be life.

"Y'ALL ARE some pathetic ass bitches. You really helped him kidnap me *knowing* that he's in love with me?" I taunted the both of them from where I sat, tied to a chair.

"I'm hoping that he kills your ass and if he don't, I sure will," China expressed with disgust. "She's only here because she knows her baby daddy is in love with you. Everybody loves little miss Kristen. You make me fucking sick."

"Don't speak for me. I'm only here because that crazy nigga in the other room has been beating my ass ever since he found out who my child's father is. I didn't want to be a part of none of this crazy shit." Both of these hoes were dumb. I mean, the dick was cool, but it wasn't enough to be out here kidnapping bitches. The door creaked open and Kane came in.

"Get out! I need to talk to her."

"Oh no, you won't be in here with her alone," China objected. Chloe did as she was asked and moved around the two and out of the room. All that could be heard was his hand going across China's face." **Whap!**

"Getcho stupid ass out this room. You not running shit in here. Go tend to the damn baby," he chastised. For the first time, I looked around the room I was sitting in. This asshole had bought me back to the old town home we once shared. She scurried out of the room, making sure to close the door behind her. He focused his attention back on me.

"What are you tryna prove by fucking up my life, Kane?"

"We wouldn't be in this predicament if you would just

come back to me. All this shit is *your* fault, Kristen. Maine getting arrested, Ant's blocks getting raided, and your shop getting torched. That's all on *you*. Oh, and not to mention, you got me fired." I looked away when he mentioned his job. "I ain't mad at you, mami. I was getting tired of the job anyway."

"Kane, you have two women who seem to want you right outside this door. Why can't you leave me alone?"

He kneeled down in front of me and went to rub my face, causing me to jump back. "You're **mine,** Kristen. I've come to the conclusion that there's no me without you. It's about time that you come around to the idea." He kissed my forehead and walked out the same way he'd come in.

"Ahhhhh!" I refused to go down without a fight, so my back was gonna have to get in line and get in line quick. I figured it'd be best to use Chloe to get out of this situation. She looked scared and I believed her when she said Kane had been beating her ass. I saw the remnants of a black eye. China, on the other hand, was so content with being second best, there was no getting through to her. I was gonna get outta here before Ant even had to come get me.

Ant

My brother being locked up had my head fucked up. I felt like I was failing in my responsibilities. Although I wasn't the one to blame, it didn't make the situation no better. Finding out from Rel that it was Kareem who was in on the set up with Kane had me hunting for him harder. My blocks were so hot, I had to shut shit down and focus on the record label, solely. Good thing I had Kris in my corner keeping me grounded.

The new artists I had signed went right to work on their projects and their mixtapes were in heavy rotation just as Maine's was. I signed two R&B artists and another rapper. I was coming out the gate hard, letting the other established record companies know we were a force to be reckoned with. Besides working and ensuring Maine was good till he came home, I had Bre around Kris more. She got so excited when I told her we would be hanging with my girlfriend. Chloe wasn't feeling it, but I made sure to introduce the two. There was an open line of communication that Kris herself had offered. I, on the other hand, didn't give a fuck about how Chloe felt. Especially since she wanted to keep seeing Kane even after I put her up on game.

After all the bullshit that went down with Maine, I called her immediately after I got to him to see if she knew Kane's whereabouts. She claimed she didn't know. I didn't believe her, so for the last six months, I made sure to have someone sitting outside of her place around the clock to watch who went in and came out, so far nothing. I knew there would be movement at some point, so I didn't mind lamping until then.

The day had been a long one and I was headed to Taj lounge to meet up with Kris for dinner. I texted her before I left the studio, but she didn't respond. Odd for her because she knew what was going on in the streets and the last thing I needed was to be worried about her, too. She had told me earlier when she came by to check on me, that she was going to stop by the shop to pick something up before dinner. It had been a few hours since I last heard from her.

Making a detour, I headed in the direction of the shop to

see if she was there. The block didn't have too much traffic and pulled up, the shop appeared closed. I don't know what prompted me to look further, but I did. Using the flashlight on my phone, I flashed into the window and saw her Louie bag in the middle of the floor.

My hand hit the glass because I knew something was off. Dialing her number again, it rang three times before going to voicemail. Jumping in my car, my tires screeched as I sped in the direction of Chloe's house. She was gon' tell me something. It was a good thing Bre was at my mom's house in case I had to put my hands on Chloe tonight.

I couldn't get out the car fast enough once I made it to her building. Banging on her door, I waited for her to answer. When she didn't, I started to bang again, but my phone rang.

"Yo'."

"**Yo' Ant, it's me, B. I meant to call you earlier to let you know that Chloe left out and it looked like she was with that detective.**" If I could have come through the phone, I would've punched this dumbass dead right in his shit.

"**You just telling me that now, B? What the fuck do I pay you for?!**" I barked before hanging up on his simple ass. Going through my recent calls, I pressed Chloe's name and the phone rang four times before she answered it.

"**He..he..hello,**" she stuttered.

I pinched the bridge of my nose before speaking. "**Chloe, where you at?**"

"**I'm out, why? Is everything okay with Bre?**"

"Chloe, I'm going ask you again, where are you?" My voice more stern than before.

"I'm out, Antwon. Look, I gotta go. Kiss Bre for me." She hung up abruptly and I knew immediately that she was up to no good. I couldn't go and tell Kaia her sister was missing with the state she was in. And I damn sure wasn't about to tell her mom or Heaven. Hitting up my tech guy, I gave him Kris's number to track her phone. He let me know that he needed someone to pick up her phone when I called and for them to stay on the phone for at least a minute to track it.

I tried it but got nothing. I hung up with his assurance that he was going to try other methods of tracking her and keep me posted. I was gon' kill Kane with my bare hands, that I could guarantee. I knew that Chloe would need to come home at some point, so I went back downstairs and sat in my car to wait for her. I didn't like the way I felt without my girl. We had become close as hell throughout this whole ordeal and to know she might be laid up somewhere hurt had me on edge.

I waited in my car for hours and it was almost two in the morning before Chloe pulled up on her street. I didn't even let her get inside of the building before I hopped out of the car. I hemmed her up against the wall by her shirt.

"Why you fucking with me, huh?" Her eyes got wide as saucers as she fought to remove herself from my grasp.

"Let go of me, Antwon."

"Where the fuck is Kane? And before you think about lying, you better reconsider."

"I don't know where he is, and I don't know where yo' bitch is either." That made me loosen my grip on her. I'd never mentioned Kris's name.

"What you just say?"

"I said, I don't know where Kane is." Her voice was low this time, so I went about another approach.

"Chloe, I don't know what type of shit you into with this dude, but you don't wanna go down this route with me. I swear to you there's no coming back and you don't wanna be an enemy of mine."

"What's so fucking special about her?! Here you are threatening me over her, and Kane is willing to risk it all just to be in her fucking presence. You even have my damn daughter attached to that bitch!" She yelled out with her arms waving wildly in the air. Pulling her to my car by her arm, I pushed her into the passenger seat. She was breaking, so I knew I could get more information from her.

"Chloe, where is he holding Kristen?"

"At his townhouse, Upstate. You better hope his other girlfriend hasn't killed her before you can get there. I'm *over* this shit. He's been going upside my damn head for the last few months." Learning that he was abusing her pissed me off and as much as I wanted to say it was her fault, I couldn't.

Any man putting his hands on a woman needed to be six feet under.

"He trusts you, so I need you to help me get her back. I have never asked you for anything but to be a good mother to Bre. You gotta help me with this, Chloe. I love her."

Kaia

I tried to keep up the charade as best as I could while Maine was down, but I was tired. I needed him home asap or I was going to lose my mind. Five months ago, I laid back on the table at the doctor's office, in a gown, on the annoying paper I kept tearing at due to my nervousness. My mother and sister were in the waiting room, waiting for me to come out. The visit was for my scheduled abortion. I had prolonged it long enough and felt it was time.

When I told my mother that I was pregnant, she immediately took me to the hospital where she worked to get my blood drawn. She didn't trust the store-bought tests as there were many cases of false positives. There wasn't anything false about that blood work, though. I was six weeks pregnant. I could tell she was disappointed and I could've sworn I seen tears in her eyes. I knew she wanted better for me, hell *I* wanted better for me.

I went through every emotion possible on that table before the doctor came in to suck the baby out of me. I wanted Maine to be there to hold my hand and tell me things would be alright. I wanted him to tell me that it wouldn't change the course of our relationship. I wanted so desperately to hear him say those words, but they had my baby locked up like a caged animal, and I was forced to handle it alone.

"Good morning, I'm Dr. Ross. Kaia, right?" The doctor asked with her hand out for me to shake. I felt a little relief that a woman would be doing the procedure.

"Yes, nice to meet you," I spoke in a low voice that matched my heavy heart.

"You're gonna be okay, sweetie, I promise. I know this is a scary time, but you got this. I know you've been asked since you got here, but I'm going to ask you again. Are you sure that you want to terminate this pregnancy?" She looked me dead in my eyes as if she could sense my uncertainty. I'm sure it was radiating off my body by now. And if the pieces of paper that were now on the floor was any indication to how I was feeling, she would know I wasn't sure.

I responded with what I thought was the best decision. "Yes, I'm sure."

"Okay, you indicated that you don't want to be sedated. Are you sure about that as well?" I nodded. I felt like I should be up to experience the pain to know the predicament I never wanted to put myself in again. "Okay, lets began. This is nurse Tanya; she's going to be assisting. Now you're going to feel a little pressure, that's just me checking your cervix and then we're going to start the procedure."

*I felt her hand go inside of me and tensed up. She tapped my pelvis for me to relax and I did a little. The tears stream down my face and all I could think was, **I couldn't go through with it.** I had thought of all the pros to getting the abortion, but I never sat back to assess the cons. What if this abortion ruined me for life and I couldn't have another child? What if something went wrong and I died on the table right here, right now?*

"Stop!" I yelled out and the doctor looked up at me. "I can't do it, I can't do this." She slid back on the chair she sat on and pulled off her gloves.

"Get dressed Kaia, we'll talk once you're done."

When I went out to my mom, she had a look on her face like she already knew what I had decided. I broke down in her arms and she held me like a baby. I didn't feel like she loved me any less for wanting to keep my baby, but I'd rather have her cuss me out than for her to be as disappointed as she was. She still hasn't come around to the idea, but she made sure she was at every appointment with me if Kristen couldn't make it.

Mase wanted to strangle Maine, especially after finding

out that he was locked up. He was also upset because I was his baby girl, but he knew that I was going to step up to the plate and be the best mother I could be. He catered to my every need and even snuck me unhealthy snacks when my mom wasn't around. Mecca and Shanice were hype about being aunties and wanted to spend every free minute they had with me. I, on the other hand, just wanted to be up under Maine. Out of the six months he had been in jail, I probably cried for four of them on and off.

I hadn't heard anything about Kandice, but I was sure she had her baby seeing as though she claimed to be three months a while back. That's something that was also weighing heavy on my mind. If he was in fact the father of Kandice's baby, I didn't know if I'd be able to handle it. I didn't want anything to do with Kandice, but I knew if the baby was his, I would have to deal with her.

Today was one of those days where all I did was cry. It didn't matter how many bags of Sour Patch watermelon candy Mase snuck me, today just wasn't the day for me. I laid in bed rubbing my belly and going through old voice notes between Maine and I, putting the phone to my belly so that the baby could hear their daddy. Only Kristen and my mom knew the gender. I wanted to wait until Maine came home to find out. I was holding onto the hope that he'd be home before the baby was born.

"You in here crying again, Kaia?" Shanice asked, peeking into my room before stepping in fully.

"Ain't nobody crying and don't say that shit too loud before my mom hear you. She said if she hears me in here crying again, she gon' go down to Rikers and break Maine out herself." Shanice laughed and I giggled through my tears.

"Why don't you go see him?"

"Girl, his ass banned me. All I have to look forward to is his daily phone calls. He hasn't called today, though."

"Since when you start listening to what he say? Get you and my niece dressed and let's take her to see her daddy."

She didn't have to tell me twice. I rolled myself out of the bed and threw on a pair of jeans, a t-shirt, and my Balenciaga sock sneakers. Grabbing my Helmut Lang hoodie, I pulled it over my head, careful not to mess up my bun. After washing and moisturizing my face, I was ready to go.

"Okay, come on." I rushed out in front of her and stopped to kiss my mom and Mase.

"Where you rushing off to?" My mother inquired.

My first thought was to lie, but I changed my mind. "Sha is gonna take me to see Maine."

"Oh, good. You tell him to hurry home so you can stop crying all the time." Mase laughed and threw me a pack of candy.

"I told you to stop giving her that shit, Mase." I ran out before she could take them from me and secured myself in the passenger seat.

"Girl, quit running before you hurt my niece." Her and

Mecca swore up and down I was having a girl. I secretly hoped so, too. "Are you nervous?"

"Yes."

"Is it because you haven't told him about the baby?"

"Yeah. I mean, I'm sure he's going to be happy that I didn't go through with the abortion. On the other hand, I know he's going to be pissed that I didn't tell him."

Shanice nodded. "Yeah, well, I get that. But check it out, if you get in there and he start going off, just rub your belly and bust out crying. He gon' feel bad instantly."

I laughed and shook my head. "You stupid."

"Girl, do that and watch it work."

After a 45-minute drive, we pulled up to Rikers and parked in the visiting area. I went to get out but Shanice stayed put.

"You not going with me?"

"Girl, no, I don't wanna be a third wheel on the outside, I damn sure don't wanna be one on a jail visit. I'll be right here when you come out. I gotta catch up on my reading anyway, so I brought my iPad. Tell him I said to hold that shit down." She smiled and shooed me away. This was her plan all along. I swear I loved my friends.

The whole check-in process was enough to make you say fuck it and leave. It didn't help that there was a rude ass lady in the front checking everybody in. Her face turned all the way up when I told her who I was here to see. I didn't know what that shit was about, but I left it alone. I was a ball of nerves while I waited to be called for my visit. I didn't know whether or not he was going to be upset that I disregarded his wishes, but at this point, I didn't care. I needed to see my man. I wanted to see his reaction to my baby bump that was visible through my hoodie, too.

"Umm, excuse me," the lady snapped. I looked around to see who her unprofessional ass was talking to. "Yeah, you, Phillips, right?" I walked over to the desk.

"Yes, that's me."

"You can go ahead on your visit." She had a smirk on her face that I wanted to address, but she wasn't worth my time. I was patted down and led into the visitation room. The nervousness I had was replaced by excitement now. The guard pointed to a table in the corner where Maine sat engrossed in conversation with a woman and something in her hands. Her back was towards me, and Maine was so focused on her, he didn't see me coming.

I sped up my walk and once I was in front of them, it became clear that the woman was Kandice. And she had a baby, *their* baby in her hands. The baby had Maine's eyes, those eyes said it all. She gave me an evil smirk while Maine sat on stuck with his eyes rested on my stomach.

"This why you didn't want me to come?"

"Baby, nah, it's not like that. I swear I didn't know she was coming today. You kept the baby?" He went to touch my stomach, but I backed away. Kandice's smile dropped at the mention of me being pregnant.

"You know what, y'all deserve each other. Two fucking frauds. I wish y'all the best." I turned on my heels and walked to the front, never looking back as he yelled my name.

"Kaia, Kaia!" I stormed out, pass the messy ass intake person who was smiling. These bitches were sick and lonely.

"What the hell? I know visiting hours ain't over. What happened?" Shanice asked as I snatched the passenger door open and got inside, slamming the door behind me.

"I hate him!" I screamed, busting out in tears. Life just had a way of shaking shit up when you least expect it.

To be continued...

Did you enjoy the read?
Let us know how much by leaving us a review on Amazon and Goodreads.

PREVIEW

Keep reading for a preview of...

Snatched Up By A Hitta

By Nai

CHAPTER 1

"Hurry up, Tae. You not moving fast enough." Katori rushed her brother in a hushed tone as they raided the 7-Eleven for the third time this week. It was late and she wanted to get home, but the stop was necessary.

Usually, Dontae was quick, but today his mind was preoccupied, and he couldn't stay focused. Katori picked up on it and at first, she told herself that whatever his issue was he'd better put it aside because business had to be handled, and getting caught was not an option. Seeing that his pace hadn't changed, she took the book bag from him and pulled out a five-dollar bill from her pocket.

"Here," she practically forced the money into his hand, "grab whatever and keep the clerk busy. I can't have you zoned out over here."

"Tori, I'm—."

Katori held her hand up, signaling for her brother to stop speaking. "We'll talk about it when we get outta here. Go head." Shooing him with her hand, she sighed, annoyed that she'd now have to do both of their jobs.

Filling up Tae's book bag and her Coach tote enough to make her content while at the same time not making it obvious that she was raiding the store, Katori made sure to glance up every now and then. Though she had tasked Tae with keeping the clerk busy, she always kept her eyes on everything and everyone. Slick as ever, she proceeded to calmly walk to the front of the store and gestured to Tae that she was making her exit.

Now, had it been any other customer, Katori was almost positive that the clerk would've asked to see her bags. Always prepared with a plan B, she made sure her plan A was clutch. Hence the reason why whenever she was out *five-finger discount* shopping, she dressed the part. With Fall making its debut, she couldn't be as sexy as she normally was, so she had to settle for a pair of tight, True Religion jeans that hugged her hips and made her ass sit up just right. The words FUCK OFF written on the front of her graphic tee that she cut low enough to expose her ample breasts expressed her entire personality. On her feet were a pair of high heeled shoe boots, and she wore a cropped leather jacket to complete the look. She'd long ago realized that her stacked body and attitude allowed her to get over with most men. Danny, the store clerk, was one of them.

"Have a nice day, beautiful," Danny called out as she went to push open the door to exit with Tae not too far behind.

"Yeah, you too, Danny," she responded without bothering to turn around.

Once outside, Katori and Dontae walked across the busy intersection of the Grand Concourse to the bus stop. While they would normally talk after hitting a store, they both waited for the bus in silence. Dontae was still in his head while Katori mentally calculated what she could make off the day's haul. She sold the snacks to the single mothers where she lived for half price, making it so that pocket change was never an issue for her or Tae. She also boosted kids' clothing and would sell those items as well.

Katori wasn't your normal booster, though. Her clientele was strictly single mothers who wanted quality clothing for their kids but couldn't always afford it. Whatever they needed, she made it happen, all while maintaining a full-time job. She was a hustler at heart.

"I still don't get why we hit this 7-Eleven when you know that nigga Danny will give you the stuff for free. Shit, he'll even give you his check just for some conversation," her sixteen-year-old brother let out.

"Well, I ain't selling conversation. And him giving me something would make me indebted to him and we know that's not how I do things." Katori handed Tae his book bag which he threw over his shoulder.

"You mad at me?"

Katori shook her head. "No, I ain't mad. A little annoyed, but not mad."

"Aight," Tae responded and looked away.

The bus pulled up and they boarded. Tae used his school-issued MetroCard and Katori used the same school-issued card, only she'd bought hers off of one of Tae's friends who decided he had better things to do than be tied up in someone's classroom for eight hours. The bus driver gave her a nasty look that she returned before following her brother to the back of the bus with her head held high. Katori wasn't afraid of getting over on any part of the system. The way she saw it, they got over by hiking up the bus fare when they wanted and never keeping the means of transportation up to par.

At 23 years old, most would say that Katori had a chip on her shoulder. Her response to that would be that life had made her the cold bitch she appeared to be. Starting with her being thrown into the position of parent after her mother had died in a house fire three years ago to the day. Katori's mother, Rena, and Tae had been home asleep when a fire broke out in their building. While making sure Tae got out to safety, Rena suffered the brunt of the flames that had accelerated and succumbed to her third-degree burns at the hospital.

That night, Katori had been out at a friend's house when she got the news of her mother's passing. The pain crippled her to the point where she didn't think she'd make it to the hospital, but she knew she had a responsibility to her then thirteen-year-old brother. She'd made it to Dontae in time to flee the hospital before DSS could get a social worker involved. There was no way in hell she'd have her brother be raised by strangers when they had family, or so they thought. The Vincent family had shown her that she and Tae were all they had when no one jumped at the chance to take them in after learning about the tragic loss of their mother.

After the funeral, Katori overheard her aunts going back and forth about who didn't have enough space to accommodate any more people and who couldn't afford it. It was crazy to Katori, seeing as her mother had opened the doors to her three-bedroom apartment plenty of times to different family members in need. Having heard enough of the bullshit, and not one to bite her tongue, Katori made her presence known.

"Y'all ain't gotta worry bout me or Tae. One thing about it and two things for certain, I'm gonna make sure we straight."

Those were the last words she'd spoken to her aunts or any of the family for that matter. Katori never told Tae the real reason they ended up staying with her boyfriend, Rob in his one-bedroom apartment as opposed to one of their aunts' homes. She also didn't let her ill feelings interfere with him having a relationship with their younger cousins. She just kept her distance and lived her life.

"Tori," Tae called her name.

"Hmm?" She answered, without looking up, locked in on

a game of Bingo Cash. If there was a way to make some money, she would explore it.

"I gotta talk to you about something." Tae's normal confident tone was filled with uncertainty that Tori picked up on. Putting her phone away in her pocket, she gave him her undivided attention.

"What's wrong?"

Tae took in his surroundings and decided that the semi-crowded bus wasn't the best forum to have the conversation he needed to have with his sister.

"We can talk about it when we get to the crib."

"You know, I really hate when you do that. By the look on your face, I can tell it's serious, so I'll wait this time." Whatever was going on, they'd long ago decided that they'd hold each other down through whatever.

After a few stops on the bus, an argument with a man standing directly over her, and pushing through a crowd of people who decided to post up near the exit, they finally made it to Rob's apartment. The place they'd called home over the last two years. Katori appreciated him giving them a place to lay their heads, but she'd outgrown both Rob's home and the relationship.

Things weren't the same between Katori and her first love and hadn't been for some time. In the beginning, when she came to him about her and Tae not having anywhere to go, he put a key in her hand without so much of a discussion. He'd developed his own bond with Tae over the years and there was no way he was about to see his girl and her brother out on the street. They moved in and with Katori having a job and her side hustle, she offered to kick in on half the rent, but Rob wouldn't accept it. Knowing how independent his woman was, he proposed that she pay the cable bill and keep the groceries stocked. She agreed and they lived in harmony as a little family for two years.

Things became strained once Tae turned 16. All of a sudden it was, *that lil' nigga eat too much,* or *he gotta play the game all night?* And whatever other complaint Rob could think of. Katori knew what was up though. Rob's real issue was that after many talks about their future, she had decided that she didn't want the baby he so desperately wanted her to carry. For Katori, life was hard as it was taking care of her little brother and making sure the both of them were straight. She knew that bringing a child along for the ride would only add on more to her already full plate. Katori was committed to doing things in excellency and in her mind's eye, if she couldn't give her baby everything life had to offer, including her time, she would rather wait.

So, after many arguments and standing firm on her decision, she saw the changes. Not one to sit on her hands and refusing to live in discord for too long, Katori became distant and went into plot mode. Between working as a receptionist at a dental office and her hustle, she was closer to her savings goal every day.

"I'm gonna hop in the shower and when I get out, be ready to lay all your burdens down, little brother," Katori said, while sticking her key in the door and turning it. Pushing the door open, an eerie feeling came over her, making her step backward and on Tae's foot, causing him to yell out.

"Damn, Tori! You just gon' step on my—." Tae went silent when a masked gunman turned the corner and pointed a gun directly at Katori's forehead.

"Come in," they heard someone say from a different place in the apartment.

"Close the door," the gunman instructed Tae, who slammed it closed and mugged the guy hard. The gunman returned the look under his mask but silently respected the young kid's

position. Katori took one step so that she was right in front of Tae. Even though the gun had her terrified, she was gonna protect her brother at all costs. "Walk."

She moved slowly and made sure that Tae was right behind her. "We don't—." Katori went to speak, and her words got caught in her throat seeing Rob tied to a chair with his head hanging to his chest. Despite the turn their relationship had taken, Katori wanted to reach out for him, but the fear made her stand still.

"Katori, right?" The same voice that told them to come in

spoke and Katori turned her head just as he came into view. The first thing she noticed was his height. He was very tall and his aura exuded confidence. Her eyes then zeroed in on the Louis Vuitton bag in his hand, and her heart dropped knowing that it held her whole $8,000 savings. "It's cool, you don't have to answer. My beef ain't witchu or your brother. I'm not sure if you know what ya man is into, but he made a move on some territory that I'm sure he knew was off-limits, right Rob."

Rob didn't move, but Katori knew he was alive. From where she stood, she could see his chest rising and falling. As the guy made it in front of him, he lifted Rob's head and Katori could hear Tae whisper, *oh shit,* from behind her. Rob's face was a swollen, bloody mess. Katori surmised that he had gotten into a situation he couldn't talk himself out of this time. She had so many questions, starting with how this man knew about her and most importantly, how did he get his hands on her savings.

CHAPTER 2

Katori was well aware of how Rob made his money and made no noise about it in the years they'd been together. The money he made selling pounds of weed kept him shelling out thousands to her over the years, dripped in designer, and recently, a roof over her and her brother's heads. In the time he'd been doing his thing, never had his occupation reached the home front until tonight. Wise enough to know that this kind of thing came with the territory, she opted to remain quiet even though she really wanted to let the unwanted visitor know that he had her shit.

"Rob, is this the bag you were talkin' bout?" The man held her bag up in the air. It was hard for Rob to see with one eye swollen shut and the other on its way. "Bossman, you gotta talk to me or I'ma have my boy put a nice size hole in ya head. Is this the bag?"

Katori hoped that he said no, but to her disdain, he gave the opposite answer. "Yea," he let out, his tone low.

The guy opened the bag and pulled out one of the rubber band stacks. He shook his head in disapproval before tossing the money back in the bag and zippering it up. "This is a start. However, judging by the many sales you've made on two of my blocks over the last few months, you, and I both know this ain't gon' cut it. So, what do you propose?" He turned and posed his question to Katori who wore a confused look.

"What do I propose?" Katori reiterated the question.

"Yeah. I mean, this is your bag, right? And I didn't pull that fact from the sky. It has your name engraved on the inside, ma."

Again, Katori went mute. Not because she didn't have anything to say, but because she had put two and two together and she was steaming. Rob knew exactly what he was doing when he told the guy to get that specific bag. He'd somehow known all along that she had money stashed in there. It only put her mind in overdrive, thinking how long he may have known and why he hadn't mentioned it to her.

"The way I see it," the man spoke again, "yo man would rather give up your money, instead of giving access to his. And I don't know how you feel about it, but the shit is pretty fucked up to me. Especially considering the position he holds in the streets as this *real nigga*. Don't seem like a *real nigga* move to me at all. What say you, Tae?"

"Leave my brother out of this," Katori voiced through gritted teeth.

"Respect." The guy put his hand on his chest, apologetically. "Rob, it seems we have ourselves a little issue. See, the last thing I wanna do is take yo girl's money, but at the same time, you know I ain't come see you personally to leave empty-handed." Pulling a gun from his waist, he cocked it back and put it to Rob's temple. "Give me what I came here for and stop wasting my time. I have better shit to do and I'm tryna have a *No Body Count October.* Don't fuck that up for me."

"That's... that's all I..."

"He has a stash in the cushions of the couch," Tae blurted out, making Katori whip her head in his direction. Tae looked past her and at the guy calling the shots. "I helped him put it up, it's in there." He figured his confession would buy them some time and Rob would be grateful for his attempt to save his life.

However, Rob cut his good eye in Tae's direction, seemingly unhappy with his outburst. And if looks could kill, Tae would be a distant memory. Mystery guy tilted his head towards the gunman behind Tae and he pulled out a switchblade. Making his way to the couch, he cut through the cushions. A slice through each one and there the bills were, nestled within the cushion stuffing.

"See how easy shit is when people just cooperate. You

mind grabbing me a bag to put this in, Tae?" The guy requested casually.

"I'll get it," Katori volunteered, locking eyes with Rob who looked like he would break down crying any minute.

"Whatever works for you, love."

Rushing off to the kitchen, Katori reached down under the sink to grab a garbage bag. Standing back up, her hand went for the drawer where they kept the knives and kitchen shears. She put her hand on a butcher knife and something in her told her to look up. When she did, she met the guy's eyes. He shook his head, and she closed the drawer slowly. Heading back into the living room, she handed the bag over and in exchange was given hers.

Relieved that her savings was back in her hands, she went back to where Tae stood and waited for what would happen next. Throwing the last of the bills into the bag, the first gunman nodded to the mystery guy. Without a second thought, he picked up one of the throw pillows to use as a silencer and sent a shot to Rob's head that prompted a shriek from Katori. Tears freely left her eyes as Rob's head dropped forward.

"Let's go."

"Wait, what?! No. We're not going nowhere with your crazy ass."

"Cool. Stay here with the body and let me know how it goes when the police get here and throw him," he pointed to Tae, "in the system."

"You just killed—."

"A snake ass nigga. You can come with me now or get wrapped up in more of his bullshit."

"More? What the hell are you talking about?!" Katori raised her voice.

"I'll explain in the car," was the only response she was given. "Wipe down everything we came in contact with then make it look like a robbery," he said to his counterpart before walking past Katori and Tae. "You don't have long to decide. I'm parked across the street, in the Prius. I won't be there for long."

Katori heard the front door close as her eyes lingered on Rob's motionless body a few seconds longer. The mystery man's counterpart seemed oblivious to the whole scene as he moved around Katori and Tae, trashing the place. Feeling her arm being tugged on, she averted her gaze.

"We gotta get outta here, Tori," Tae expressed with urgency. Seeing Rob get knocked off right in front of him messed his head up, but even at his young age, he knew the magnitude of the situation if they were to stick around any longer. Tae couldn't bear the thought of being separated from his sister. Especially not with the recent turn of events in his life that he'd yet to divulge to her.

"Grab what you can and put it in your duffle bag. I'll figure out the rest," Katori said with her feet still planted.

"I ain't moving till you move," Tae let her know, matter of factly.

Sighing, Katori took Tae's hand and stepped over the overturned coffee table.

"Y'all got ten minutes," the accomplice alerted the two. There was no time to really pack anything but their necessities. Given the severity of the situation, they'd have to figure everything else out as they went along.

As Katori rushed to pack, she thought about the last conversation she had with Rob. It was heated and they'd exchanged a few choice words that she felt there was no coming back from.

"I don't know what the fuck you mad about, I ain't saying shit that ain't true," Rob argued while lighting his kush-filled blunt.

"That's the thing, every time I become quiet you take it as me being mad when I'm really just processing." Katori wasn't quick to speak when in disagreement, especially when it was about a sensitive topic. She had realized from the start of the conversation that it wouldn't end well.

"Yeah, processing another bullshit ass excuse to give me as to why you don't wanna carry my seed," Rob spat. "That's what you were put on this earth to do. And don't give me no bullshit excuse about taking care of Tae either. That lil nigga is a grown-ass man."

Katori examined her French manicure and shook her head. "If you think talkin' to me crazy is going to convince me to want a baby, you got another thing coming."

"After all this time, Tori. Me putting a roof over...you know what, fuck it." Taking a pull of the weed, he let it settle in his lungs before exhaling.

Although Katori was offended that he'd mentioned opening his doors for her and Tae, she wouldn't admit it out loud.

"Lemme ask you a question, Rob. Did you let me and Tae move in here just so you could hold some shit over my head?"

Again, he inhaled and then exhaled, blowing smoke in her direction. "What kinda lame as shit is that to do?"

Katori shrugged. "I don't know. It's starting to seem that way, though. Understand this, if I ever gave you the impression that I needed you to be my savior, that was my bad. I wanna make it clear right here, right now that me giving you a baby will not be a reward for your good deed. I wasn't ready when you first brought it up and I'm not ready now."

"Heard you. You won't hear shit else about it. Just remember, what you won't do, the next woman will." His voice was laced with disdain that Katori made note of.

The interaction further solidified the ending of the relationship.

"You ready?" Katori asked Tae as she walked out into the hallway with what she could fit in her Louie luggage and the knapsack that held her savings. She'd traded her heels for a pair of New Balance to move around better.

"Yeah, just grabbing this picture of mommy." Tae grabbed

the framed picture of their mother from the closet where he kept his belongings and put it in his bag.

Heading back to the front of the house, the once organized living room, courtesy of Katori's love for cleaning was now in complete disarray. Rob's body was still in the same position. With the scene already etched in her brain, Katori didn't take another look as she and Tae made their way to the front door.

"Don't touch the doorknob with your hands," the accomplice said to them.

She wanted to say something smart in response, but let it go. Tae stepped around her and used the sleeve on his hoodie to open the door. It was a good thing that Rob lived in a building where people stayed to themselves and minded their business for the most part. While sometimes it was a blessing, it was a curse when someone really needed help. Glancing to the left and right, Katori waved for Tae to come out. She wanted to do her best to avoid being seen leaving the apartment.

They decided to take the steps down to the lobby. Leaving the building, she spotted the Prius immediately. The mystery guy had kept his word by waiting on them. It was the one thing that kept her moving towards the car and not making a detour up the block.

"You sure about this?" Tae asked his sister, undoubtedly leery about the situation at hand as he walked beside her.

"No," she answered honestly. "The only thing I'm sure of

is that I'll never let anything bad happen to us," Katori spoke with conviction and Tae nodded, already knowing how his sister was coming about him. And she meant every word, even though it seemed morally wrong.

As they got closer to the Prius, Katori went around the back of it and snapped a picture of the license plate. Although she was blindly going with the mystery man, she would make sure to get the license plate info over to her best friend. Opening the back passenger door, they were halted by the guy's voice.

"I ain't no Uber, ma. One of y'all sit up front," he stated.

"Can you pop the trunk?" Katori requested, ignoring his statement. The trunk opened and she and Tae tossed their heavier bags inside. Tae got in the backseat while she slid in the passenger, clutching her savings. "Look, I don't know what you got going on or even what you have planned for us but know that I'm not gonna make it easy for you if it comes down to it."

The mystery guy gave Katori a full once over with his dark brown eyes. She felt uncomfortable under his stare. It was like he was searching for something, and she didn't like it. His stare made her feel vulnerable.

"I don't have any intention of hurting you or your brother if that's what you're getting at. You'll understand why what happened back there was necessary soon enough." He started up the car and pulled off.

How he'd justify killing Rob was questionable to Katori.

She knew something was up and she couldn't shake the feeling that leaving with this man was sure to open up Pandora's Box.

Available Now

On all online retail book platforms!

ALSO BY AUTHORESS NAI

Elevated By His Gangsta Love

Bossin' Up On The Plug

Bossin' Up On The Plug 2

In The Trenches With My Hitta

In The Trenches With My Hitta 2

Stealing A Queenpin's Heart

Stealing A Queenpin's Heart 2

A Piece of A Hustler's Heart

A Piece of A Hustler's Heart 2

A Thug's Love Mended My Heart

A Thug's Love Mended My Heart 2

A Summer To Remember With My New York Bae

A Summer Fling In New York

His Hood Love Gave Me Life

His Hood Love Gave Me Life 2

My Thug, My Sanctuary

Thug Kisses For Christmas

For The Love Of My Savage

Charge It To The Game

Charge It To The Game 2

A Summer To Remember With My Hitta

Snatched Up By A Hitta

Santa Sent Me A Real One For Christmas

OTHER BOOKS BY

<u>URBAN AINT DEAD</u>

Tales 4rm Da Dale

The Hottest Summer Ever

Hittin' Licks For The Holidays: Atlanta

By **Elijah R. Freeman**

Despite The Odds

By **Juhnell Morgan**

Good Girl Gone Rogue

By **Manny Black**

Hittaz

Hittaz 2

Hittaz 3

Coldhearted

By **Lou Garden Price, Sr.**

Charge It To The Game

Charge It To The Game 2

A Summer To Remember With My Hitta

Merry Trapmas: Ice & Frost

By **Mia Sky**

Charge It To The Game 3
By **Nai**

The Swipe 2
By **Toōla**

A Gangsta's Last Kiss
By **Mia Sky**

Pretti & The Beast
By **P. Wise**

BOOKS BY

URBAN AINT DEAD's C.E.O

<u>Elijah R. Freeman</u>

Triggadale

Triggadale 2

Triggadale 3

Tales 4rm Da Dale

The Hottest Summer Ever

Murda Was The Case

Murda Was The Case 2

Murda Was The Case 3

Hittin' Licks For The Holidays: Atlanta

STAY CONNECTED

Follow
Elijah R. Freeman
On Social Media
FB: Elijah R. Freeman
IG: @the_future_of_urban_fiction